■ □ ■ □ ■

THE PROPHECY AND OTHER STORIES

■ □ ■ □ ■

WRITINGS FROM AN UNBOUND EUROPE

The Prophecy

and Other Stories

DRAGO JANČAR

Translated from the Slovene and with an
introduction by Andrew Baruch Wachtel

NORTHWESTERN UNIVERSITY PRESS
EVANSTON, ILLINOIS

Northwestern University Press
www.nupress.northwestern.edu

The stories included here were originally published in Slovene in the following collections: "Two Photographs," in *Smrt pri Mariji Snežni* (Ljubljana: Mladinska Knjiga, 1985); "The Specter from Rovenska," "Joyce's Pupil," "A Sunday in Oberheim," and "A Tale About Eyes," in *Prikazen iz Rovenske* (Ljubljana: Cankarjeva Založba, 1998); and "The Prophecy" and "The Man Who Looked into a Tarn," in *Človek, ki je pogledal v tolmun* (Ljubljana: Mladinska Knjiga, 2004).

Printed in the United States of America

10 9 8 7 6 5 4 3 2 1

Library of Congress Cataloging-in-Publication Data

Jancar, Drago.
[Short stories. English. Selections]
The prophecy and other stories / Drago Jancar ; translated from the Slovene and with an introduction by Andrew Baruch Wachtel.
p. cm.—(Writings from an unbound Europe)
ISBN 978-0-8101-2578-0 (pbk. : alk. paper)
1. Jancar, Drago—Translations into English. I. Wachtel, Andrew. II. Title. III. Series: Writings from an unbound Europe.
PG1919.2.A54A6 2009
891.8'435—dc22

2008048246

♾ The paper used in this publication meets the minimum requirements of the American National Standard for Information Sciences—Permanence of Paper for Printed Library Materials, ANSI Z39.48-1992.

■ □ ■ □ ■

CONTENTS

■ □ ■ □ ■

INTRODUCTION: HISTORY AS IRONIC JUXTAPOSITION

Drago Jančar (born 1948) is unquestionably the leading Slovene prose writer of the past thirty years, and one of Europe's most celebrated writers and intellectuals. His career has been exceptionally varied; he has published novels, short stories, plays, film scripts, and essays. A visible opponent of the Yugoslav Communist regime (which jailed him for three months for dissidence in 1974), Jančar was an influential supporter of and polemicist for Slovenia's decision to declare independence in 1991. Over the years he has been awarded numerous Slovene and European literary prizes, including the Jean-Améry Prize for Essay Writing in 2007, the Herder Prize in 2003, and the European Short Story Award in 1994. His books have been translated into some twenty languages.

Although perhaps better known as a novelist and essayist, Jančar excels as a short-story writer, and he has published eight book-length collections of work in this genre. The earliest of the stories translated here was written in 1985 ("Two Photographs"), while the most recent date from 2003. Although they come from different periods of Jančar's career, they are linked, I would argue, by two constant, almost obsessive themes: the first, which grows from the work and thought of Jančar's great Yugoslav predecessor Danilo Kiš (1935–89), is that history is essentially an ironic process; the second is that this irony is best conveyed by a focus on the process of perception, particularly visual perception.

Jančar's overt homage to Kiš can be immediately appreciated with a glance at the opening lines of the story "Joyce's Pupil," which starts with the story's conclusion, in a narrative voice that echoes Kiš's: "This story will end with a mob dragging an old man with a weak heart—a retired professor and former law school dean—out of his house and loading him on a wheelbarrow as they cry out in anger and derision. He will be pushed through the winding streets of the old town toward the river, to be dumped into its rushing, freezing current. The final lines of the story will be cried out in Slovene, in its upland, alpine dialect; mocking cries will resound on the street along which the wheelbarrow, with the bouncing helpless body on it, will rattle."

A reader familiar with Kiš's oeuvre will recognize a stylistic echo of the first lines of "The Knife with the Rosewood Handle," the opening story in *A Tomb for Boris Davidovich:* "The story that I am about to tell, a story born in doubt and perplexity, has only the misfortune (some would call it the fortune) to be true. But to be true in the way its author dreams about, it would have to be told in Romanian, Hungarian, Ukrainian, or Yiddish; or, rather, in a mixture of all these languages."* The connection is through the hypertrophied concern with the proper language necessary to tell the "true" story (a story of death in both cases) as well as through the narrator's seeming ironic detachment, which in fact conceals a forceful and continual engagement with and critique of historical events.

Unlike Kiš, however, who does not find anything particular about the Serbian or Yugoslav experience (though it can be claimed that he finds the Diasporic Jewish experience paradigmatic), Jančar is especially, though not exclusively, interested in exploring the relationship between modern Yugoslav history (and Slovene history in particular) and larger world historical processes in his work. Thus, the longest story in the collection, "The Specter from Rovenska," follows the adventures of a Slovene stonemason who becomes a soldier in the ill-fated army of Emperor Maximilian I of Mexico (the younger brother of the Austrian emperor Franz Joseph). "Two Photographs" juxtaposes the tragic fate of a father and son, the former killed by Yugoslav Partisans in the immediate aftermath of World War II for his membership in the Slovenian Home Guard (a military force that col-

* Danilo Kiš, *A Tomb for Boris Davidovich,* trans. Duška Mikić-Mitchell (Champaign, IL: Dalkey Archive Press, 2001), 3.

laborated with the Axis occupiers during the war and whose members ranged from far-right sympathizers to nationalist anti-Communists; after the war many escaped to Austria but most were deported back to Yugoslavia, where many were executed without trial), and the latter, a left-wing sympathizer and sometime Communist organizer, killed by the right-wing Argentine government during the dirty war of the 1970s. "A Tale About Eyes" is set in Croatia and the United States, while "The Prophecy" contrasts a Yugoslav army base in the 1970s with the postwar realities of the former Yugoslavia.

Nevertheless, many of the stories remain Kišian in tone and theme. For Kiš, whose Hungarian Jewish father died at the hands of the Nazis during the war and who spent much of his life in Communist Yugoslavia, the clash of left and right was the ideological key to understanding European history in the twentieth century. He dealt with the crimes of Fascism in his early novels, most powerfully in *Garden, Ashes* and *Hourglass,* and with Communism in *A Tomb for Boris Davidovich.* In "Two Photographs," Jančar sharpens the issue by bringing the conflict between these ideologies (what the narrator terms at one point "the third world war between the left and the right") together in a multigenerational family drama. Like Kiš, Jančar tells his story through a distanced, narrative voice, which provides an almost cinematic perspective on the events. The narrator seems to be omniscient, yet there are key facts to which he is apparently not privy. Thus, for example, he does not know which of two stories explaining the reasons the Polish Argentine Witold Ozynski betrayed the movement is true.

What he does know, however, is the immense power of sight, eyes, and visual imagery to stimulate the memory and imagination. In "Two Photographs" it is the photographs themselves, clutched in the hands of the almost mute old woman who is wife and mother of the two martyred protagonists. The snapshots freeze time at a particular moment, and that moment becomes the only reality onto which she can hold. Regarding the newer photograph, the narrator remarks: "Until the moment when a push of the button tripped the camera's shutter and captured his smile, preserving him in a snapshot sitting on a wicker sofa in a garden somewhere wearing a light-colored shirt with his legs crossed, until that moment we can say nothing that would help us to understand the arc of Gojmir Blagaj's life, the surprising and powerful events that were to follow, events that the old local priest, in all his rustic simplicity and gravity would call a devil's brew." The existence of this artifact, however, is apparently sufficient to prompt the entire story about Gojmir's subsequent life and death.

About the earlier photograph, the narrator comments: "With unusual gravity, the silent eye of the camera in the officer's hands captures the faces of the soldiers at that instant." The silent eye of history will reappear in many of the stories in this collection. It is the main focus of "A Tale About Eyes," which opens with the contrast between two sets of eyes, those of the Croatian Ustaša leader Ante Pavelić in the literary recollection of Curzio Malaparte: "At first glance I saw only the bright gleam of his eyes, like the shimmer of a river's surface." These eyes are juxtaposed to those of Albert Einstein in the recollection of his doctor: "His eyes were angelic. You had the feeling that they knew everything in the world." The eye of history follows us even in stories that are not, strictly speaking, historical, such as "The Man Who Looked into a Tarn." Here, it swallows up the title character Jože Mlakar, an ordinary Slovene who becomes by accident of fate a lightning rod for all issues in postindependence Slovenia from the first time he looks into a camera's lens: "He somehow sensed the power of those millions of pairs of eyes that were looking at him through that single eye, that magical eye, and he did not see but rather sensed the vortex of that eye swallowing him up in its depths." Finally, it is an exchange of glances that sets Ivan Glavan and the future Emperor Maximilian on their parallel roads to Mexico. As Glavan would later recall, "The emperor was close by and they could have understood each other with a single glance, with the same kind of glance they had once shared in a far-off place called Rovenska."

In addition to their focus on perception, the stories presented here are distinguished by Jančar's deft sense of historical irony, presented with an economy and laconism, which lends his stories a forward drive that will be, I believe, extremely attractive to the Anglophone reader. To some extent, this irony is produced by the juxtaposition of the extreme passion characteristic for the actors in the story with the distanced and measured, nonetheless wry tones of the narrator-historian. But the irony is also a function of the repetition and patterning within the historical events described, a patterning which, to be sure, in most cases goes unrecognized by the central actors. Thus, Boris Furlan can have no idea of the consequences of the English lessons he takes from an eccentric Irishman in Trieste, nor does the future Emperor Maximilian realize the power his bumbling words will have on the imagination of the Slovene stonemason Ivan Glavan. Even the biblical "prophecy" of the classics professor on an obscure Yugoslav army base in the 1970s stands in a highly ironic relationship to the events that would unfold in the 1990s, precisely because it turns out to be true, or close to true. All we have, it seems, are the literary equivalent of various characters' fifteen minutes of fame, described most poignantly in the story titled "The Man Who Looked into a Tarn," but expressing, at least implicitly, the truth thought by the main character in the final line of "The Prophecy": "But all has passed; today all those ancient kingdoms and their armies no longer interest anyone, and by tomorrow we too will be forgotten and no one will understand these stories."

THE PROPHECY AND OTHER STORIES

■ □ ■ □ ■

THE PROPHECY

ONE PEACEFUL AUGUST MORNING, ON THE INNER DOOR OF A BATHroom stall, Anton Kovač saw an inscription that made his blood run cold. The loud echoes of commands and the clopping of thick-soled boots against asphalt could be heard from the distant parade ground—the mustering ground was called the circle, although it was hard to figure out why since it was shaped like a large square; the new recruits were practicing marching under the hot sun. Here in stall 17 it was cool and quiet, just as it was in the whole row of empty stalls that had recently been cleaned. Anton Kovač was an old soldier, which meant that he had only about a month to go before his tour was up. He worked in the library and was no longer required to drill, which was why he did not begrudge himself the chance to sit on the toilet in the middle of the afternoon reading the newspaper. He hadn't read the inscriptions on the bathroom walls for a long time. When he was still a pheasant—that's what new recruits were called, no one knew why—he'd eagerly read the vulgar thoughts, the names of girls from far-off places, those bitches who were sleeping around while the guys here were pissing blood, groaning about the number of days left to serve, all the messages liberally ornamented with sexual organs. Since he was a professional reader, a librarian, he'd thought for a while about jotting down the most inspired graffiti and putting together a small anthology of bathroom literature, which is to say, an anthology of all the yearning for civilian life, an anthology of jealousy, melancholy, quickly formed petty hatreds, conceits, mockeries, and comments.

But he soon dropped the notion. The Balkan military vocabulary was colorful and varied, but it had one archaic leitmotiv which could be called "fuckin'," sometimes used literally but more frequently allegorically. Everybody was fucked, from mothers and sisters to brothers and grandfathers, from dogs and cats to abstractions such as sadness and joy, from vegetation to things to objects; someone had even written, "Fuck your house's address." The quantity and monotony of bathroom creativity had eventually begun to bore him. And that is why when he was able to spend a few minutes in that space, when he was no longer a pheasant, he returned to the normal occupation of civilian life: reading the newspaper. He never took a book into the stall; that seemed improper somehow, and not just because he was a librarian. He was a passionate reader for whom books, at least the majority of books, were receptacles of spirituality, chalices of wisdom, vessels of intoxication, and newspapers were simply not.

When he lifted his glance from his newspaper that August day, he suddenly saw the inscription amid the drawings and the graffiti; it did not lack the well-known leitmotiv, but its message was so unheard of, so blasphemous, and so dangerous that the blood ran cold in his veins. Almost by the wall, on the right-hand side of the door, in blue pen in uneven letters and in Serbo-Croatian, someone had written something that Anton Kovač would never forget and that he would translate into Slovene years later:

> You'll eat grass, King of Yugoslavia
> Donkeys will fuck your fat ass.

His first thought was: *Out of here. Get out of this place as quickly as possible.* It seemed he was hearing the hellish ticking of a time bomb that could destroy his life. He wanted to fly out the door when he stopped himself. If anyone saw him coming out of stall 17, he would be a suspect. He listened carefully. He could hear nothing from the corridor except the dripping of water from a broken faucet—and the beating of his heart, which was up in his throat. From the circle he could hear terse commands and the pounding of boots on asphalt. It sounded like bursts of machine-gun fire; the pheasants did not yet know how to march. It should sound like a single step, not like machine-gun fire; that is how sheep walk. A single step, he recalled the motto written on the barrack wall: "We are all Your step." A new command brought the marching in the circle to a halt. He heard the young corporal telling the recruits how to move their feet and that they should bang their boots onto the ground "so that your balls fall out."

Anton Kovač walked to the aisle with the sinks; it was empty. He would have preferred to run, but he calmly washed his hands and then forced himself to walk slowly and lazily, as if to let everyone know that an old soldier was passing by, always moving slowly, with loose straps and his cap stuck into his belt and not on his head. He avoided the yawning soldier on guard duty who was dozing against the gun rack.

When he entered the library he yawned with boredom, as if nothing had happened in his boring soldier's life for a long time. And he let himself relax. For the moment it seemed to him that he was safe. The senior officer who ran the library was fiddling with the dial of the crackling radio receiver, and his colleague, Professor Rotten, who like him was finishing out the last month of his tour, was typing away.

"How goes, Anton? Did you finish reading the paper?" Rotten asked without even looking up.

Anton Kovač wanted to ask him to walk over to the shelves so that he could tell him what he had just read. Recently he'd become quite friendly with this professor, this Belgrader by the name of Rotten. Both of them found the last month of service hard to take; they had gone into town together a couple of times to listen to a café singer in a short skirt and to get a bit drunk. Rotten was a serious young man, a quiet academic with impeccable military and library discipline. He sometimes loosened up on Sunday trips into town and would silently down a few shots of brandy. It seemed to Anton Kovač that it would be all right to tell him about the horrifying thing, the time bomb that was waiting in the cool, quiet of stall 17. But at the last moment he decided not to. If two people know something, everyone does.

"Fine," he said. "Just fine, as always."

He sat down at his desk and began to write book titles down on catalog cards. "It's hot," said the sergeant, who turned off the crackling radio, walked over to the window, and opened it. The pheasants were still out there, endlessly thumping the asphalt with their boots.

"Sing!" called out the corporal down there on the circle. The lone, pure, and resonant voice of a single young pheasant rang out a song to the rhythm of the marching boots, the "Hymn of the Artillerymen":

"We're artillerymen
The army has called
To guard all our borders
And Marshal Tito."

And the chorus of recruits loudly called out the refrain:

"Tito's a marshal
A genius is he,
He's in command
Of our splendid army."

Anton Kovač asked himself how many times he'd sung that song before he'd mastered the art of marching. A hundred times? He thought he'd sung it so many times that he no longer knew the meaning of the words he had spoken. Now he suddenly knew how portentous those words were, how horribly at odds they were with what he had read a little while earlier. And he thought about the bold, insane person who had dared to write them. Anyone who would dare to do that could easily place a bomb in the barracks.

He slept badly; every time the duty officer in the big bunkhouse woke a new soldier for watch duty he would bolt upright. In a half-awake doze he saw an invisible hand writing letter by letter on the bunkhouse wall the lines "you'll eat grass, King of Yugoslavia . . ." The other part of the writing was so coarse that Anton Kovač did not allow himself to see it; every time it appeared in his mind's eye he blinked his eyes and began to think feverishly. The second half of the horrifying graffito, that vulgar expression of hatred toward the supreme leader, was by itself more or less harmless, as its tone was in keeping with all the variants of penetration that covered those same walls from top to bottom. Anyone could have written it. But there was something mysterious about that grass. He recalled a bad joke he had heard once in a bar: A beggar is sitting by a road along which big-shot government officials are traveling and he's eating grass. The first official stops and gives him a tenner, the second comes along and gives him more money, and then the white-uniformed marshal stops in his black Mercedes, but instead of giving money, he asks, "Why don't you go eat over there where it's clean and fresh?" No, no good. "You'll eat grass . . ." Why? If we know who the king of Yugoslavia is, why was it written in such a fancy, almost biblical tone: "You'll eat grass, King of Yugoslavia." Maybe it means that you'll be killed with your face in the grass? Terrifying thoughts overcame Anton Kovač that night. And the worst was that he might be suspected of the act. He had often used stall 17 because it was the cleanest. Now he knew why. Anyone who had been there even once must have avoided it thereafter. Only he was stupid enough to have kept going in there every morning. Like a murderer who keeps going back to the corpse until it's found. He imagined that he was already under suspicion. Of course, anyone could be under suspicion, but if anyone could be suspected or even accused, then that anyone could easily be him. It was only after four in the morning, when the last soldiers returned from guard duty, that he managed to catch a couple of hours of sleep before reveille. In the morning he involuntarily looked to see who would go into stall 17. While he was there, no one did.

He spent the next few days in the library in a state of incessant, low-level anxiety. He sensed that something was going to happen: an officer from the counterintelligence service would open the door, step inside, and ask, "Who wrote that?" But nothing of the sort happened. Peace and quite reigned in the library. The officer twirled the radio dial as he always did when he was there, either that or he was off taking care of his own affairs. His friend Professor Rotten was a silent type who was generally bent over his papers. In those August days he was already preparing his university classes. He kept a copy of the Old Testament underneath a pile of papers and would pull it out and begin taking notes as soon as the officer closed the door behind himself. He was preparing to teach a seminar on biblical themes in world literature in the fall semester. Professor Rotten's real name was Milenko Panić, but in that artillery base in southern Serbia no one had known this for a long time, and everybody called him Professor Rotten, or even more frequently just Rotten.

He had received his new name soon after joining the army. He was a pheasant, no more than a month into his service when once, during the morning muster, Major Stanković came to a halt in front of him and fixed his glance on the open button on the pocket of his shirt. Two pens were sticking out of his left pocket. Major Stanković was a gruff but pleasant man whose heavyset figure might have seemed dangerous to some—indeed he might have looked to them like a pit bull preparing to attack—but in fact he was a good-natured sort, always ready for a joke. And so the soldiers liked him.

But even so, Panić was ill at ease when he stopped in front of him.

"What's that?" the major asked, pointing to the two pens sticking out of his pocket. Panić shrugged his shoulders and the major shifted his glance to the young corporal who was standing next to him, paralyzed with terror at having to answer for the undisciplined appearance of his soldier.

"I asked, What's that?" the major repeated.

Panić replied stoutly, "Two pens, comrade major."

Silence fell. It was not a good answer, as everyone could see that there were two pens and the major could easily get angry. But he did not get angry; he just stared at him for a time.

"I thought they were some sort of military decoration," he said slowly.

He chuckled, the relieved corporal laughed loudly, and the whole long row of soldiers joined him.

"What do you do in civilian life, soldier?"

"He's a professor," the corporal answered.

"I asked him," said the major.

Panić looked around, somewhat abashed as about a hundred soldiers and several officers waited for his answer. He explained that he was a classical philologist; he'd studied Latin and ancient Greek.

"What do you need them for?" the major asked.

Panić did not reply.

"*Why, those are rotten languages,*" the major guffawed, and all the soldiers in the ranks joined him so loudly that there was an echo off the walls of the barracks. Panić blushed. *Rotten,* that is to say, decayed languages were dead, unnecessary, and funny, just like the first, rotten Yugoslavia that had to collapse so that the new Socialist Yugoslavia could appear. Panić wanted to say that it was not proper to speak this way about Latin and Greek, about things to which he had chosen to devote his entire life. But then he realized that he had no desire to hear more jokes from the amused major. He swallowed his saliva. Satisfied with himself, Major Stanković continued to walk along the row of soldiers while Professor Milenko Panić just stood there amid the men, alone and humiliated, a professor of decayed languages.

By the afternoon he had become Professor Rotten, and by the evening, when some of the men wanted to needle him, he had become just Rotten, and so he had remained.

He never became reconciled to this new name, which brought him no end of difficulties. Anyone saddled with such a funny name, which, worst of all, he received to general merriment, automatically becomes the target of daily mockery, general familiarity, and the butt of little jokes. Who doesn't know how to take apart a gun? The professor of decayed languages. Who'll wash the latrines this morning? Professor Rotten. And the angrier his face became, the more fun everyone had with Professor Rotten. One night they even made him do the bicycle. This was a favorite nighttime trick of soldiers. They would stick a piece of paper between the toes of a sleeping person and light it on fire. When the hot flame got close to the skin, the leg began to twist, and the closer the flame got to the toes the faster went the "bicycle." Only when the pain got really bad did the person wake up with a surprised look and glance around in amazement at the laughing faces. Rotten had had to put up with the bicycle on a number of occasions, precisely because he was a professor of rotten languages. He was only able to get a bit of respite when he and Anton Kovač were assigned to the library. There he threw himself into his studies. And every time the officer who ran the library and its piles of Marxist scholarship, Partisan historiography, and patriotic literature walked out the door, he would pull his copy of the Vulgate from his heaps of papers and begin eagerly to lose himself in the mysteries of the text. This shortened the hours and days that remained before the end of his term; with every page he turned, he got closer to his home and farther from the laughingstock Professor Rotten.

His calm was infectious. For a few days Anton Kovač still trembled every time the door to the library opened, but then, alongside this tranquil person, he returned to his life in the barracks library and waited for his demobilization. Slowly he began to forget about the dangerous writing in the bathroom, and he also stopped waking up and seeing the invisible hand writing letters on the bunkhouse walls. On his morning visits to that place, which he could not completely avoid, he noticed that no one ever used stall 17. One afternoon he marshaled his courage and opened the door to the stall. The message was still there. He leapt away as if from a snake.

August turned into September, and only fourteen days remained for him to serve. On Sunday he and Rotten went into town, did some pub-crawling, and listened to Gypsy music. With the sound of trumpets echoing in their heads, they returned to the base in a petulant mood. It was the penultimate Sunday.

And now the penultimate Monday began. It began with running down the corridors and sharp commands that cut through Anton Kovač's head, which was still a bit dizzy thanks to Sunday's brandy and Gypsy trumpets. He squirmed through the mass of bodies that were looking for their boots in the corridor and headed for the toilets. The bathroom was locked and the guard who stood in front of the door said that the plumbing was out and that he should use the bathrooms in another part of the base. Anton Kovač knew the plumbing was not broken and that when something like that happened they never guarded it. He headed for the library, but he met Rotten in the corridor on the way.

"The library's closed," he said. "We've all got to line up."

"What's up?" Anton Kovač asked cautiously.

"What's up?" Rotten said. "Some nasty shit's up, and only two weeks before we get out of here."

They tightened their belts, quickly laced up their boots, and at the last minute, Anton Kovač took the two pens out of Rotten's shirt pocket and stuffed them in his pants pocket. It would not be good to have good-humored Major Stanković stop in front of him again this morning. Then, amid the crowd of men stampeding in the corridor and hopping down the stairs, they made their way out onto the parade ground.

An ominous silence reigned on the circle as the last of the men rushed to join their units. A group of officers, led by Major Stanković, emerged from the officers' quarters. The duty officer called out: "Atten—shun!" The major's heavyset figure, which usually radiated good nature and readiness for a joke, now seemed gloomy and dangerous. He walked up to the small reviewing stand, and the officers ranged themselves behind him. An intelligence officer, a captain, tried out the mike: "One, two, three, testing." Then he withdrew, leaving room for the commanding officer. The major stepped slowly to the microphone, biting his upper lip, and for a few moments it seemed that he was thinking about what to say. A cold September wind from the nearby hills blew over the heads of the silent soldiers.

"We are the Yugoslav People's Army," the major said in a soft voice that the loudspeakers made almost metallic.

"We guard this country and its legal order. Our supreme commander is Marshal Tito, who led this army triumphantly through the Balkans in bloody battles for liberty and victory."

He fell silent, allowing the soldiers to digest these phrases.

"And in this army there are people who do not respect what we hold most holy. Even worse, people who are prepared to sabotage brotherhood, unity, and our freedom."

The breeze carried his words to the last rows of soldiers. Hands behind his back, he took a couple of steps on the podium.

"We no longer have kings," he continued unexpectedly. "Kings fell along with the old and rotten Yugoslavia."

He looked at the intelligence officer, who was as white as a sheet. And he spoke as if that officer was directly responsible.

"Counterrevolutionary graffiti has appeared in our barracks; that is all that I can say for now. Anyone who could write something like this"—and Anton Kovač knew very well what he would say—"anyone who could write this would be capable of planting a bomb in wartime. Or turning his gun on one of his comrades. We will not allow this. We will track these individuals and groups down and we will court-martial them. You will receive further instructions in your units."

The duty officer called out, "At ease."

The investigation began. To start with, the soldiers of each unit were asked to sit at the classroom desks. A young corporal with supple, twitching fingers placed a piece of paper and a pen in front of them. He lit a cigarette and recited a prepared speech. It was an old fairy tale that begins with a description of a grassy place across which rides a man on a donkey, and there are donkeys around eating grass. And then a king goes by accompanied by his retinue; the words *grass, king, Yugoslavia, donkeys, you will eat* appeared a number of times in it. And every time Anton Kovač got to one of those words his hand shook. *You shouldn't shake,* he thought, *because a handwriting expert will be asked to say whose hand shook while writing the word* donkeys. Rotten, completely calm, was sitting right next to him and writing down the sentences the corporal was dictating very slowly and repeating frequently because not everyone in the room could write very well. Anton Kovač wondered how many of the guys knew what was going on. Stall 17 was clean and empty; many people avoided it. He wondered whether Rotten knew, and he was sorry he hadn't asked him. That would be one more attestation that he hadn't done it. No one who wrote that could have asked a friend whether he had also seen what he had seen. But then the intelligence officer would start asking why he hadn't reported what he'd seen. "Perhaps you don't love Marshal Tito as much as everyone else does?" And in fact Anton Kovač did not love him. Anyone who loved him would have nothing to fear; he would quickly have reported that hostile and disgusting activity. But Anton had remained silent and therefore had become an accessory.

That night the horrible inscription appeared again on the bunkhouse wall, and in his rambling dreams it seemed to him that his eyeballs were broiling and that he could not hide from what was being projected from his eyes.

The next day there was no talk about uncovering enemy individuals or groups on the base. At breakfast he heard they'd arrested an Albanian whom they had found in possession of live ammunition that he had apparently stolen while on guard duty. Someone said he'd be put before a firing squad, bang, right on the spot. But Anton Kovač knew that these were merely the usual words young soldiers bandied about to make the time go faster. At the circle, just before the morning muster they heard that an unscheduled military exercise was being organized. That sounded a lot more likely. But no one said anything about why the investigation was happening at all.

In the morning an intelligence officer came by the library and asked them whether they'd seen anything unusual, any soldier who was behaving strangely. He asked what books had been taken out and who had taken them. The officer in charge of the library was clearly more frightened than either of the two soldiers, and he answered quickly. Nothing could happen here because he never leaves the library. The officer looked Anton Kovač in the eye and asked him how frequently he left the library and whether he went to the bathroom. "I do go," he said, his heart beating quickly, "but always with the sergeant's permission." The sergeant confirmed this, and that satisfied the intelligence officer. Then he took some sheets from the pile of papers that lay in front of Professor Rotten. Anton Kovač knew there was a Bible underneath. Rotten was calm, gloomy, and motionless. When the officer removed the final sheet there was nothing underneath. The professor had removed the Old Testament and his notes in time. Anton Kovač relaxed. They really didn't need a new scandal because of a Bible; there was enough going on already.

In the evening there was an alarm; they were turned out in full kit, and under a cold rain blown in by the mountain winds they had to march some ten miles to the rifle range. There they had to put on gas masks and hurl themselves into a swamp. They didn't get back to the base until the next morning and fell right into bed. But at ten in the morning they were up practicing their marching to the "Hymn of the Artillerymen." No one was allowed to stay in the classroom or the library. Anton Kovač began to think that the ten days that separated him from the end of his tour would last forever. He knew that in exceptional circumstances the term of military service could be extended.

The sun came out again at noon, and during the rest period he lay on the grass behind the mess hall, stretching his sore legs that were no longer used to marching. He lit a cigarette, looked up at the clouds, and wished to escape quickly from what was coming, perhaps tomorrow. He imagined the heavyset Major Stanković walking across the circle, leaning toward him, and saying, "Civilization is waiting for you in the depot; you may go." *Civilization* was another word that was not very clear to him; it meant civilian clothes that had been sent from home. But those were only pleasant midday thoughts brought by the clouds that rushed into the Balkans from the valley of the Morava River on their way to either the Aegean Sea or the Black Sea.

At five in the afternoon they were again chased out onto the parade ground. They marched around the circle and sang: "Tito's a marshal, a genius is he . . ." And the more the boots crunched, the more he asked himself, *Who wrote that? Who will be unmasked?* And although what they were looking for, what diversion, had never been stated, and although none of the soldiers had admitted to seeing anything on the bathroom walls, Anton Kovač sensed that the words were flashing before the eyes of each of the marching men. It was like at a funeral, when one suddenly cannot keep from laughing; at every step some letter from the bathroom walls shone. For every marshal about whom they sang there was the grass that the king of Yugoslavia would eat. For every genius there was a donkey that would fuck the commander in chief in his ass (a terrible thought), or in his fat ass (an even more terrible thought). During the guard duty he had to do again by the armory where the 155 mm cannon were kept, when the stars were just twinkling out in the sky and the first light was coming over the mountaintops, he wished that the culprit would be found. *Let him be captured to put an end to this uncertainty; let him be caught and brought before a court-martial.* Later Anton Kovač would be ashamed of having had those thoughts; a court-martial was no joke, but at that time he was such a nervous wreck that he would have been glad to see the fool court-martialed, sent to jail, anything. After all, thanks to him he was stuck on the base. Rotten would miss a semester, if not a whole year. *How was it possible,* he thought angrily, *how was it possible for this unknown writer to issue such a wild challenge inside this army that was feared by all, even by the citizens of the country who also loved it because they feared it, just as they feared and simultaneously loved its commander, marshal, and genius?*

Although it seemed to him that he would never get away, it turned out that he was able to leave the base only a few days later than had been scheduled. It seemed that they had first of all to investigate those whose tours were about to end. There were quite a few and things got held up. But then time passed with a speed that astonishes us only when we stop.

For Anton Kovač the years passed faster than those final days on the base in southern Serbia when it seemed to him that each hour lasted an eternity. Particularly because of his fear of it, that writing lodged itself deep into his memory. Only once he started to tell his friends about what had happened to him in the far south. They had a great laugh, but he never told the story again because they were most amused by the fact that he and no one else had been sitting terrified with a newspaper—it had been the Belgrade paper *Politika*—holding up his open pants with his hand. People are malicious; they are most often willing to laugh at someone else's predicament, incompetence, or general unhappiness in unfortunate circumstances, like when they do the bicycle. Who could really understand Anton Kovač and his distress in those last days of his army tour? And so he was happy to forget the whole thing; he wanted to forget it. And besides, there were new events; the world was out of joint for a while. The marshal died and soon after so did the country itself. The army that was supposed to protect it collapsed, and no one marched on the circle singing the "Hymn of the Artillerymen" anymore. When he saw burning Balkan villages on the television screen and heard the roar of 155 mm cannon, he sometimes thought about the officers of that glorious and triumphant army. *Where were they now? What uniforms were they wearing?* He recalled the young corporal with the supple fingers (*where was he lighting cigarettes now?*), the lazy sergeant from the library (*he was probably retired*), and Major Stanković (*whose soldiers was he commanding, to whom was he speaking from his podium?*). But it was all so far away, and when the wars were over, it all became farther away and even more nebulous, and it lodged deeper in the mists of memory.

One day on television Anton Kovač saw a man with earphones on his head sitting in front of a tribunal and denying that he was guilty of killing civilians. His face seemed somehow familiar. Then the camera showed that same man wearing his army uniform. His figure was heavyset and his sleeves were rolled up. With a pleasant chuckle he was telling some miserable civilians that nothing would happen to them. A group of officers and soldiers was standing near him, and then they forced those people with their bundles onto some buses. Anton Kovač suspected that he'd seen that face; *was that not the good-natured, though sometimes gloomy and dangerous Major Stanković?* Then his hair was black, but now it was gray. And then for the first time, as if an enormous wave was washing over him, that whole set of events, in every detail, came back to his consciousness from the depths of his memory. He was not shaken by the televised clips, but he was shaken by that old fear from the cold corridors of the army base far to the south.

In the middle of the night, half asleep, he again saw the invisible hand writing on the wall. And he thought that the bathroom inscription had been some kind of prophecy. A prophecy? *Mene, Tekel*? Now he was wide awake. He got up, got dressed, and in the middle of the night went to the library, where he worked as a cataloger. He turned on all the lights in his office, and all the lights in his head went on as well. He searched for a Bible; he knew where *Mene, Tekel* appeared. In the book of Daniel an invisible hand wrote "Mane, Thecel, Phares," as it is translated in the Vulgate. He riffled the pages with a shaking hand: "And his heart became like that of an animal. He came to live among wild donkeys and they gave him grass to eat . . ." The king of Babylon was kicked out of his palace; he had to live among donkeys, eat grass, and he had an animal's heart. And it went on: "The Babylonian king . . . before him all humanity had quaked, the peoples and nations had shaken in his presence. He could kill anyone he wished and he could keep anyone alive; he could raise up anyone or cast them down."

The king of Babylonia, Anton Kovač thought. *Of course, of course, that was the message: the king of Yugoslavia was the king of Babylon.* "Then they brought in the gold vessels that had been taken from the temple, God's house in Jerusalem. And the king, his notables, his wives, and his concubines drank from them. They drank wine and worshipped gods made from gold and silver, bronze, iron, wood, and stone."

And now, now he saw him, the professor of rotten languages walking through the corridor in the middle of the night, or perhaps in the middle of his workday, in the army library with his ballpoint pens stuck in his shirt pocket. He greets the guard in the corridor nonchalantly, goes into the bathroom and down to the end of the row of stalls, sees that no one is around, undoes his belt just in case, and takes out his pen. "And at that moment a hand appeared and it wrote on the plaster wall of the palace . . . *Mene tekel upharsin,*" which means, as Professor Rotten knew very well, "God has numbered the days of your kingdom and brought it to an end. You have been weighed in the balance and found wanting, and your kingdom will be divided among the Medes and the Persians." And he also knew the fate that the king of Babylon had been promised in the book of Daniel: "He will live among the wild donkeys, he will be given grass to eat like a cow, and his body will be washed by the dew of heaven." *How he'd hated that fat and dissolute king; how my friend, that silent librarian, professor of rotten languages, had hated him. He wrote a prophecy about him on the walls of a bathroom in southern Serbia; he couldn't do it except in a vulgar version, mostly to avoid being caught but also so that all would understand.* Writing something as terrifying as *Mene, Tekel* could be done only in the form chosen by his quiet friend Professor Milenko Panić, who could escape from himself only when he'd had a few brandies.

Anton Kovač turned off the lights, closed the library door, and headed into the night. He drove around the dark streets of Ljubljana for a long time. *Maybe he hadn't hated the king of Babylon,* he thought. *Maybe he was just getting his revenge for his petty humiliation, for the fact that he had become the professor of rotten languages, the mocked Professor Rotten. Maybe he just wanted to give them a message translated from his rotten language into their living soldier's dialect.* Anton Kovač looked into the rearview mirror: *I have gray hair, and you also have gray hair, Professor Rotten, somewhere in Belgrade or wherever you are, and Major Stanković also has gray hair; I saw him on television. Your mysterious prophecy was indeed horrible, Rotten, and true. But all has passed; today all those ancient kingdoms and their armies no longer interest anyone, and by tomorrow we too will be forgotten and no one will understand these stories.*

■ □ ■ □ ■

THE MAN WHO LOOKED INTO A TARN

ONE SPRING AFTERNOON A CASHIER AT THE MERCATOR STORE noticed a man standing in a corner near the dairy case and speaking out loud. As she'd been working there a long time, the cashier was used to all sorts of strange behavior, and so at first she'd paid no attention. Customers would sometimes repeat the shopping lists they'd gotten from their wives out loud; the bums who came in from the nearby park to buy wine and cigarettes would frequently disturb the afternoon peace in the store with their monologues. But this middle-aged man intoning disjointed sentences as if telling someone about something did not look like a bum. He was wearing a dark blue suit, had a tie on, and when he'd entered, he'd greeted her politely. Only his face was a bit scruffy; he had clearly not shaved for some time, and he smelled a bit, as the cashier later recalled, like a man who had been roaming about for some time and who had not had time to change his shirt. But that could just be a man's exterior or the forgetfulness of a traveler. Then, without picking up a shopping basket, he'd gone straight toward the back of the store, and a little later the clerk realized he was still standing there, looking up at something and speaking continuously. Then, having taken care of three or four good customers who usually came in at around that time, she went into the office to tell her manager about the talking man. Her boss just waved her away with his hand when she opened the door.

"I see," he said, without looking at her. "I've been following him for some time."

He was sitting at his desk and steadily watching one of the monitors on the wall.

"He's talking straight into the camera," he said.

In fact, because of its placement, the security camera that was mounted high on top of the refrigerator case and that covered the entire space between the shelves with its eye, projected on the screen in the office in a somewhat elongated perspective the face of the speaking man and the crisp gestures that gave emphasis to his statements.

"Weird," said the clerk. "Perhaps he's a little out of it. Though he looks pretty normal."

"Too bad there's no sound," said the manager. "I'll have to go out there to hear what he's going on about."

If the clerk and her manager had looked a bit more carefully, and had the camera not elongated the scruffy speaking face in such a strange way, they would easily have been able to recognize, easily able to see that he was Jože Mlakar, not three years removed from the time when everyone knew his face. He used to speak about the direction of our foreign policy on the evening news shows; during election campaigns he commented on the left and right deviations of party leaders, and he took part in roundtables about the working hours of grocery stores. Once he stood in front of a tank and explained that the defense of the homeland does not depend on arms but rather on the patriotism of the citizens; another time he stood on a bridge over the river and insisted that we are all endangered because of shoddy building material and carelessly calculated load limits, but most happily and most entertainingly he talked about human rights. Human rights are the foundation of everything, even more than the materials used for building bridges and their load-bearing capacity, more important than foreign policy or development strategies. Jože Mlakar carried in his breast a moral compass, as he would eloquently say every time he had a microphone in front of him and whenever the fixed eye of a camera was on him: "a moral compass in my breast and the starry vault above." Jože Mlakar was ready to do anything for human rights, even sacrifice humanity itself, or at least that segment of humanity in our homeland who failed to understand that human rights were everything and that one has to do everything for them.

His ascent into the orbit of human rights and television cameras began in those days of rupture and glory when we liberated our homeland. He never forgot (nor did he ever forget to mention publicly) the emotions that had overcome him when he spoke for the first time. That spring evening he was standing in front of the stage, where microphones were being tested. He saw the crowd of people, the crowd of resolute faces that had poured from all the streets into the main square. The first lights on the square were being turned on, the searchlights were stabbing through the evening air, and in that beautiful evening sky the stars were also beginning to appear. And he also saw the cameraman who, with a camera on his shoulder, was searching out important and not-so-important details of those historic events. The accompanying reporter kept sticking her microphone into the faces of members of the crowd, and, at the vision and the thought of the millions at home in their armchairs who were following the developing events with tension in their chests, Jože Mlakar also wanted to state his opinion. This was not merely, as he would later say many times, because he would be seen by millions, and among them his family and coworkers, but even more because he was pulled inexorably into the vortex of history. He also knew what he would say into the microphone—with a gaze directed straight into the camera, he would say, "We shall never surrender." If he had the chance, he would speak just like Churchill—"we will never give up, we will fight on the seas and on the beaches, on the fields and on the streets"—even if, come to think of it, there are no beaches in that town. Then the crowd, coming in waves from here and there, pushed him away from the microphone and the camera, so that in the end he found himself wedged underneath the stage on which the meeting was beginning.

He never knew, as he was happy to recollect later, how he found himself on the stage. He knew only that he first threw his briefcase up there because he didn't want to put it down, and then, finding himself up there also, he grabbed his briefcase and with thumping heart but steady steps walked up to the microphone that was ceded to him by one of the enthusiastic speakers. He saw that not merely one camera was following him: all eyes, all lights, and all cameras were on him. But he looked into only one of them, the one that the nearest cameraman was holding on his shoulder. The small, slightly convex surface, the deep eye of the camera literally dragged him in, as he later recollected. At that time he did not think of the millions of pairs of eyes that were behind it looking at their television sets, but he somehow sensed the power of those millions of pairs of eyes looking at him through that single eye, that magical eye, and he did not see but rather sensed the vortex of that eye swallowing him up in its depths. He said that human rights were first and foremost a moral law, and he didn't even hear his voice through the loudspeakers, or the roaring of the crowd of people, but he sensed some figures ascending to the stage, and he announced that he was going to say something that the whole world would understand because he would say it in English. From the corner of his eye he saw the figures of the security guards coming quickly toward him across the stage, and quickly, as clearly as he could, he said into the microphone, "We shall never surrender; we will never give up because this has to do with our rights." He said this through the thousandfold amplification of the loudspeakers, and he wanted to add, "We will fight on the streets and in the fields," but then a figure wearing an armband on his sleeve materialized next to him and someone said, "Mister, please come." He did not allow himself to be dragged off the stage, and briefcase in his hand as if he had done his duty, he calmly stepped away but not completely offstage. He was a bit dizzy when he again found himself among the crowd of bodies and hands that clapped him on the back.

He went to a telephone booth, stuffed a coin into the slot, and dialed the number. A moment later he heard his wife's voice.

"Did you see me?" he screamed in order to be heard over the booming music and roar of the crowd. "Could you hear what I said?"

"Have you gone insane?" said his wife's agitated voice. It seemed to him that she was sobbing. *What's going on with her,* he thought. *Why is she crying now?*

"What's the matter with you?" he said, and he thought there must be some misunderstanding.

"You're nuts," sobbed his wife. "Nuts. Don't come back home."

He simply did not understand this, and he never spoke publicly about what that evening had meant in his private life. He replaced the receiver and stood awhile in the telephone booth, his spinning head unable to process what had happened. Then he left the main square and headed for a cheap restaurant in one of the side streets of the old town, a place where he would often go to have a glass of wine with his friends after work. It was as if someone had poured cold water over him, or, better, as if he had been hit over the head with a hammer, the same head that was ringing with the proud words he had spoken to millions and even more with his wife's intolerable wailing. Of course he knew that she didn't really think he was nuts or even less that he shouldn't come home. She'd frequently used words like this before, whenever he'd called from the restaurant to say he'd be a little late. When she said, "Don't come back home," what she wanted to say was that she was in a bad mood because he was late again. But when she said it this time, it was simply too much for Jože Mlakar. He was shaken to his core. *If that's how it is,* he thought, *then I just won't go home.* When he entered the restaurant, the television was on, and when he walked up to the bar, he found not one but three glasses of wine in front of him, and again someone was clapping him on the back: "You spoke really well." After the first glass of wine his decision not to go back home if he wasn't wanted there became more definite. But after the last one, when the restaurant was closing, his decisiveness abandoned him. Where to go if not home? But his wounded soul would not give in. What kind of home was it if they thought he was nuts? Just because he had done something for the collective good, for the nation's good, and for human rights. He should have been honored rather than told not to come home, as if he had been on some kind of binge and not at a magnificent meeting. He thought he would sleep in the headquarters of the shipping company where he worked, for he had the keys in the briefcase that he was still clasping tightly. He would explain to the night watchman that he had important business, lock himself in his office, and stretch out on the couch. Let his wife, her mother, and his pimply son who told him not to come home wonder where the man was whom they had shoved over the threshold of his own home, one that he had built himself with patient economy and no little sacrifice, even helping the mason frame in the windows and lay the ceramic tile in the bath.

He headed off to the edge of town where the headquarters of the shipping company were located. The streets were almost deserted; the last meeting goers were hurrying to their hearths. He started to shiver despite walking quickly; the spring day had been warm, and he had gone to work in a light jacket. Then he stopped. What would his coworkers think tomorrow when they found him sleeping on the couch? To tell the truth he didn't care, because that evening he had burned all his bridges. His very home had been taken away, so let them think him crazy as well if they wanted to. He simply didn't feel like explaining to anyone how the magical eye of the camera had dragged him into its vortex. He went to the train station, grabbed a cab, and told the driver to take him to a hotel in a little town near the capital. He knew where to go because he used to go there with a girl whose parents kept her on a tight leash, forbade her to see him, and staked out his bachelor studio apartment. That was the same girl who was now his wife and who told him he was nuts and, worse yet, that he should not come home. Then they did not have a joint household but rather a safe haven in that little hotel where he was going. In his head he counted up the money in his wallet, enough to pay for the ride and a night's lodging, and tomorrow, ah, tomorrow was another day; now he had to do only what he had set out to do. He would hide, tell the desk clerk to keep things quiet, after all he knew how to do it. But it wasn't so easy to hide. Even the taxi driver recognized him.

"I saw you on television," he said.

"Ah," said Jože Mlakar modestly, "no big deal."

"Sure, sure," said the driver. "You spoke well."

At the hotel, Jože Mlakar fell right into bed. He was tired, and thanks to the driver's affability, even admiration, he fell asleep, somewhat less unhappy. When he half woke in the dawn light, in that moment between waking and sleep, between night and day, he saw an enormous vortex, an enormous round eye that was inexorably drawing him in with such force that he almost became scared. Then he ate some chocolate from the minibar and fell back asleep. He slept until the early afternoon, when he was awakened by a blackbird cheeping and squawking on the balcony.

When he looked at the clock he got worried. By now he should have prepared a pile of documents for customs and tolls, he saw the angry truck drivers standing outside his office waiting to be sent on their way, he saw his secretary trying to calm them down, and he saw his boss lifting the phones and slamming the doors. Jože Mlakar was not a political mountebank, of which there was no shortage at that time, nor was he the kind of person who would jump onto a stage to scuffle with the security guards, as someone who had seen last night's protest meeting on the main square might have thought. Even less was he crazy as his wife claimed, he thought sadly. He was a solid worker, never late to the office. He prepared all the necessary documentation for trucks that headed off every morning to distant lands: to Sweden, Turkey, Iran. He liked to hang around with his friends, that was all, and recently over their wine they had discussed political events—who hadn't? He did not know himself what had dragged him in front of the camera, some kind of unknown force he could not resist. But he did not regret what had happened; he was only sorry that his own family had not understood, and he was even sorrier that he was now sitting in a little hotel going through his wallet, out of which gaped an unpleasant reality: it was more or less empty. He showered quickly, with some distaste put on yesterday's shirt, and headed off to the check-in desk, briefcase in hand. He prepared himself to overcome his embarrassment and to ask the clerk, who knew him from the days when he used to sleep there with his present wife, to let him put off paying until that evening. He was afraid of humiliation, for Jože Mlakar was well known for paying his bills. But the clerk was waiting for him with a smile, his glasses resting on the bridge of his nose.

"I saw you on television," he said. "You spoke well."

Jože Mlakar was relieved. Now his head was clear, last night's dizziness had passed, and he was tempted to bask a bit in the clerk's admiration. He asked what had seemed so good, as he wasn't able to say everything.

"I didn't hear all that well," said the clerk. "We had a lot of guests."

Jože Mlakar became silent with an almost insulted air. He asked whether he could make a telephone call.

"But everyone says that you spoke well," the clerk added quickly. "You showed them what's what."

He called his office. His secretary answered quickly.

"Where are you?" she asked. "Everyone's looking for you."

Jože Mlakar was covered in cold sweat. He saw the faces of the irate drivers counting up every lost mile, all the lost money. He saw his boss telling him that he could go look for another job, one where the working day started at eleven in the morning.

"Who's looking for me?" he asked in a dull voice, because it seemed to him that he knew very well who was looking for him. But, he was wrong.

"Television, the newspapers, everyone," his secretary said in an agitated voice. "They all want to hear you."

Jože Mlakar stared at the receiver for a long time. He wished his wife had heard that, wished her mother had also, along with his son before he'd gone off to school. He heard the loud, sharp voice of his secretary through the receiver. He pulled himself together and said calmly, "Tell them that I'll be there in an hour."

Without any difficulty he got the clerk to agree to let him pay later. He headed off into the sunny spring day, briefcase in hand. He was a bit agitated because of the sudden turn of events, even a bit bewildered, but the voice he suddenly heard he would later ascribe to that particular psychological state. It was a male voice which spoke just outside his ear, quite clearly, a bit hoarse as if that of a very important person who was leaning down to his ear and saying, "These are your five minutes of fame, Jože."

He trembled a bit and looked around, but he was not overly shocked. These really were his five minutes, maybe even his fifteen minutes, there was no doubt about that. The only problem was money for the bus fare: he would have to explain quickly to the conductor that he had no money for the fare, and he felt the heavy weight of shame and all the shaken dignity he would have to swallow. He was already searching for the right words with which to explain his predicament when a car stopped next to him. As a matter of fact it had first passed him but then had come back to him in reverse. The driver opened the window and asked if he could give him a ride. Jože Mlakar nodded and sat down. As they were going along the driver said what we know.

"I saw you on television. You were speaking at the protest meeting."

"Ah," said Jože Mlakar. "It was nothing much."

They drove by a police car parked by the side of the road. The driver looked at the briefcase his passenger was holding in his hands.

"Could you put that under the seat?" he whispered.

Jože Mlakar looked at him in amazement.

"Why?" he asked.

"So it won't be found if they stop us," whispered the good-hearted chauffeur.

He thought there was no reason they should be stopped. The car wasn't going too fast, the day was nice, and even if they were stopped, why should he hide a briefcase with shipping documents under the seat.

Just before they reached the city the driver suddenly veered off to the right and took a narrow road up the hill.

"Where are you going?" Jože Mlakar asked.

"Taking a detour," said the driver.

Now he was beginning to lose his patience. Television cameras were waiting for him at his office, and he first had to stop at home to get a clean shirt. Even though it wasn't his home anymore, he thought sadly, but still the dresser with his shirts was there; there was no other way.

"Excuse me," he said with suppressed anger, "why are we taking a detour?"

"Because they're looking for you."

Jože Mlakar knew that they were looking for him, perhaps the cameramen were already setting up in his office, focusing their cameras on the spot where he would sit and deliver his statements.

"They've promised to arrest everyone who spoke at the protest meeting."

He told him that he'd be happy to take him to his relatives' house; they'd all been opposed to the government for a long time, they'd be proud to help.

His heart skipped a beat, and for a moment he didn't know whom to believe. He decided to believe his secretary.

"Just head into town," he said, "if that's where you're headed."

In a few months this pronouncement would give Jože Mlakar enormous prestige, or better yet it would augment the prestige that accrued to him by the time the historic events surrounding the liberation of our homeland had already unfolded. The unknown driver would, once freedom had been won, write letters in which he would explain how he and the speaker at the protest meeting had managed to avoid arrest because he drove him safely through the hilly streets straight into the center of town to the office where the television cameras were waiting.

Twenty minutes later Jože Mlakar was sitting in an armchair in front of a television camera. Not in his office but in the director's.

"You can't be giving interviews in that cave of yours," the director of the shipping company told him when he met him in the courtyard. "So we turned my office into a studio."

The director was aware that the wheel of history was turning, everyone knew it at the time, and he did not want that wheel to toss him off to one side, and that was why he opened the car door of the unknown driver who was shaking Jože Mlakar's hand and accompanied him to the microphone and the camera.

"That's fine," Mlakar said in a calm, almost condescending voice. Even so he was a bit nervous when the soundman pinned a microphone to his shirt, and not so much because of the filming but because of the shirt he had not managed to change and that unquestionably gave off, through the pores of his skin, a body odor redolent of last night's wine. He angrily thought of his wife because had it not been for her he would be sitting in a freshly ironed shirt, clean shaven as he was every morning. But a moment later he forgot about this. When he looked into the dark eye of the camera, everything disappeared: the director and his secretary who stood respectfully in the background; he'd forgotten the dirty shirt, the injustice he had suffered at the hands of his nearest and dearest; forgotten was the suffering of the previous evening and the unpaid hotel bill. In the distance he heard the voice of the reporter telling him that he should look at her rather than directly at the camera, but Jože Mlakar couldn't look at her. The magical eye of the camera drew him in with a mysterious power.

"Ready," said an unknown voice.

"We're rolling," said another.

He heard the reporter saying that at last night's protest meeting the speech of Mr. Jože Mlakar had garnered particular attention. She paused for a moment and said, "Here we'll dub in your speech." After a moment she continued: "Mr. Mlakar is now with us. What did you mean to say?"

"Just what I said," replied Jože Mlakar in a collected tone.

"Could you lay it out in a bit more detail?" asked the reporter, who expected that every beginning would be followed by a more detailed explanation. A few moments of tense silence followed. And then Mlakar heard not a silence but a roaring in his head, which was now empty and from which now gaped a void something like the void that had stared at him this morning from his wallet in the hotel room, and it also seemed to him that he was hearing the cheeping of the blackbird on the hotel balcony. The reporter and the director exchanged glances and got ready to cut the filming off. And then suddenly the words bubbled out of Mlakar—about human rights that were threatened despite the fact that they should not be threatened: "Injustice is being done to people, and some people who are fighting for liberty and equality are being called insane," he said. "They've taken away our homeland, injustice is everywhere, just look at the drivers who wait in front of my office, they have to get a pile of papers to do their job, and it is the same thing with students and retirees, not to mention nurses, our homeland is threatened in all these ways," he said, "and we won't give up, not on the streets or in the fields or even on the shores."

Much later, when his star was already descending, malicious tongues said that from the very beginning Mlakar had had nothing to say, although there was no doubt, added the media analysts, that he had said it with a particular conviction and decisiveness—in fact with the decisiveness of a man to whom injustice had been done—and it was because everyone else also felt unfairly treated that his words seemed so convincing. And in addition, his glance was fascinating. He always looked straight into the camera and he seemed to say more with his presentation than with his words. But that was much later. Now was the time of his ascent. And even though Jože Mlakar's pronouncement this time was not as inspiring as the words the exalted crowd had welcomed the night before, the reporter was satisfied. The producer nodded, his boss congratulated him, and his secretary even hugged him. "I never knew," she said, "that such a wonderful man was working in our shipping company office. Our Jože," she explained, "is always so modest." It suddenly occurred to her that his humility was enormous and that he was also handsome, although she had never noticed that before.

Jože Mlakar didn't hear any of this. He was looking into the glass surface of the camera's eye, which was reflecting his miniaturized image, drowning in its smooth and peaceful surface, below which was the invisible vortex of millions of eyes. He glanced into that deep tarn and felt himself dragged inexorably into it.

That evening, together with his wife, her mother, and his son, he watched his televised performance. And later, when he and his wife were alone, he said, "Well, what do you say now?"

Naturally, he didn't want to start a fight; he'd let it drop long ago, in the afternoon at least, or maybe even at the time between night and morning when he'd woken up in their hotel and eaten the chocolate bar. She didn't want to fight either. She just looked at him a bit distrustfully. There was something strange about her Jože; his eyes were shining and his gestures were jerky. What really concerned her was when he told her in confidence, only her, about having heard the voice of an enormous person on the road into town.

"How enormous?" she asked.

"Very, very enormous," Jože said, "though I didn't see him."

It seemed strange to her that he knew he was enormous even though he hadn't seen but had only heard him, but he didn't have time now to explain such petty details. After all, she didn't understand what had caused him to jump up on the stage, so how could she understand a voice that was, in the end, directed only at him.

"Go to bed," he said. "I still have work to do."

And he threw himself into such a frenzy of note taking that the pieces of paper flew from the kitchen table. He knew that his opinion would be solicited and that he would have to be ready to answer, so he wanted to be well prepared. He was not mistaken. The phone began to ring in the morning. He was invited to so many things that he had to call his office to tell them that he wouldn't be able to come in. His boss accepted this with understanding, his secretary with amazement.

In the days that followed, he was invited for interviews and to roundtables; he spoke at meetings and celebrations. Workers and farmers, retirees and students, all wanted to hear the decisive, albeit somewhat opaque, comments of Jože Mlakar. Politicians also came to see him, and they invited Jože Mlakar to join the parties they were creating at that time. But he refused their polite appeals. Jože Mlakar was no politician, or even the voice of the people; he was his own voice. If he were to have spoken frankly, he would have had to admit that he was the voice of that unknown power that came over him every time he gazed into a camera. That was why he also refused to do newspaper and radio interviews. A microphone by itself, unaccompanied by a camera, was meaningless for him, but soon there was no local television station or speaker's stage captured by television cameras on which Jože Mlakar had failed to appear. He did not go back to work in the following days, and eventually he even stopped using his overcommitment as an excuse for his absence. A film producer made a documentary about him under the title *The Man Who Began to Speak.* And indeed, Jože Mlakar was a man who had begun to speak at the right moment. And that moment stretched into months. Now one saw him in front of a tank speaking about the defense of the homeland and patriotism, now on a bridge holding forth about construction materials and about the truckers who drive on our awful roads, but most frequently and most eagerly he spoke about human rights and injustice. He read somewhere about the moral law that men carry in their breast. "In my breast there is a moral law, and above me the starry vault," he would say into the camera; and the viewers were inspired. He spoke well, they would say.

One evening when he was happily watching a clip of his long monologue on a local television station, his joy was interrupted by a telephone call. It was the desk clerk at the little hotel where, as everyone knew, Jože Mlakar had spent that now-long-past historic night in order to avoid arrest. He asked whether Mlakar intended to pay the bill. He had laid out his own money to pay it and was hoping to get it back. The matter-of-fact tone of the clerk's voice annoyed Mlakar. Because he could picture him sitting there, behind his desk with his glasses on his nose, worrying about such absurdly trivial things. Then he had risked everything, arrest and maybe even his life, and now this guy wants some money, although he'd sacrificed himself for the homeland and for the common good (including, of course, the clerk's). And he told him that. The clerk said he did not understand. And then he added acidly that he also failed to understand what he talked about on television and elsewhere, and that he was going to take him to court for the unpaid bill. Jože Mlakar was heartbroken, could not believe that people had become so petty and intolerant now that the wheel of history had turned and we had liberated our country.

But the wheel of history had indeed turned. Our homeland was free, and people began to go back to their everyday occupations. Jože Mlakar continued to appear on various television shows, now even on commercial channels, but his words and fascinating glance no longer evoked as much interest or the same powerful response. He even began to get on some people's nerves. His mistake was that he lacked a sense of measure. He appeared and spoke almost every day, and the time came when he needed to take a break—everyone knows that people eventually get weary of popular figures and they need to lay off. But Jože Mlakar could not take a break. He remained intoxicated by the camera's eye, and when he was not asked about some important question or not invited to participate in a roundtable discussion, he would call the station's offices to complain. It was all very well then, he would say in an angry voice, when the homeland was in peril and when human rights were in danger, but now they were taking away his most basic human right, the right to state his opinion. And this was happening now, when he had much more to say than when he had jumped onto the stage and, truth be told, uttered only one sentence. The last straw was when he got a call from the director of the shipping company who asked whether he was intending to come back to work. Especially when he added politely that they could not keep paying him for appearing on television. Mlakar angrily hung up the phone and devoted himself to his true calling. Now his room was full of papers, the wall was covered with Post-it Notes with quotations, exclamations, and questions all linked to problems that needed to be discussed. He had long since given up writing in the kitchen and had moved into an attic room in the family house where he had also set up a small camera so that he could practice for his appearances. But this camera did not give him any real satisfaction. It could not draw him in like a real camera behind which were millions of pairs of eyes and the millionfold power that was concentrated in the convex, mysterious glass. He rarely had any contact with his family, because during the day he was out looking for new reasons to hold forth, and at night they would hear cries and passionate phrases emanating from his garret. One morning, in a newspaper they pushed under his door, he read an article that threw him for a loop. "What Is Mlakar Talking About?" was the title of the article that a journalist had written in a mocking and even nasty tone. "Those who have nothing to say usually talk about human rights," he wrote. "They'd be better off speaking about synthetic fertilizer." Mlakar tore up the article angrily, threw the pieces into the bathroom sink, and turned on the tap. But he still had one great appearance left in him. He called the reporter who had conducted that first interview with him in the office of the director of the shipping company and asked her to invite him for an interview. "I won't speak about human rights," he began to say even before she asked him anything. And then he spoke for a long time about synthetic fertilizers, about how they were poisoning our water. He spoke a bit opaquely but decisively, as he had during his greatest hour. Some viewers understood that his harangue was a witty response to the presumptuous newspaper reporter, especially when he concluded with the thought that polluted water was also a question of human rights and that those who defended them would never give up.

That was his final appearance.

It was then, so it is said, that the president himself uttered the words that sealed his fate: "Take the microphone away from that Mlakar."

At the morning meeting of his advisers he apparently justified his bad mood by explaining that the state of the country worsened every time Mlakar spoke. That could be discerned by his popularity rating among the country's citizens. Mlakar opens his mouth and the president's popularity falls by 5 percent. One of his advisers had the temerity to note that Mlakar didn't usually speak about the president, that most recently he had spoken about the quality of lake water threatened by synthetic fertilizers.

"So what?" the president said. "We need to put an end to it."

Another adviser twirled his pencil and mused out loud that it would be difficult to forbid every reporter to stick a microphone in Mlakar's face, and that it might be better to ask the shipping company that was paying his salary to tell him he had to come back to work. That would close him down.

"Hmpph!" said the president's secretary, who was happy when her president was happy and angry when he was he was angry; now she was angry.

"He'd still keep talking," she said. "It's irrelevant."

"Take the microphone away from him," the president repeated. "And don't let him near a camera."

This was not so easy to do. Even though the ban on Jože Mlakar's appearance before any camera had practically become state policy, it was simply not effective. It was one thing to tell the editors at all the major and minor television stations that they were not to invite him to speak in front of the camera, but someone had to stop Mlakar—

and rethink the meaning of the words he had spoken at that historic protest meeting. Those words meant that he, Jože Mlakar, would never give in. One Saturday evening he appeared on a program shot at the open market. He skillfully popped in front of the camera of a naive young reporter who was idly asking consumers about their alimentary habits and began to speak about people in this country who eat salad filled with lead that comes out in automobile exhaust and that this is a threat to elementary human rights. They hardly had time to suspend the reporter before he appeared again, this time at a soccer match alongside a sports announcer. Not suspecting anything, he invited the spectator who had spent the whole first half nodding his head pleasantly right next to the broadcast booth (and who looked familiar somehow) to come inside and give his opinion. And Jože Mlakar stated that in his humble opinion they should not be playing with a single attacking forward because as a result they weren't able to do any playmaking in the middle of the field. And this deprives us fans of goals, which are the most beautiful thing about soccer, and thereby affects the rights of people to enjoy their Sunday leisure time. The announcer could see that this outburst was getting away from the subject of the soccer game, but he couldn't stop Mlakar's impressive conclusion. "And that means," Mlakar said, looking straight into the magical eye of the camera, "that this is a terrible violation of human rights, which are spoken of in international conventions, the Geneva ones and others." The commentator, who had never been much concerned with human rights, recalled to his horror that the Geneva conventions had to do with the rights of prisoners of war, and there had been no war here for some time. Then, with a shaking hand, he turned off the microphone, but the television audience could easily see that Jože Mlakar kept on talking.

The cameramen of various television stations who knew him were aware that his face was not to appear on screen anymore, and so they knew that they would have to take their cameras quickly in a different direction whenever he appeared. Some of them pitied him and sometimes they would put a camera to their shoulder in some out-of-the-way part of town and allow him to speak into it, though they did not actually record him. Others, less sympathetic, would play jokes on him in the breaks between shooting. One day, for example, a television crew got bored waiting on one of the town's bridges for a famous writer whom they were supposed to film talking about time that flows and changes like a river, with the green river in the background.

"Hey, Mlakar," yelled a cameraman who recognized him as he crept closer in ever-narrowing circles getting ready to leap in front of the poet the moment he appeared.

"Hey, Mlakar, why don't you ever sing?"

"Because he's tone deaf," said the light man.

"I'm tone deaf?" Mlakar said.

"Well, sing a scale."

"You mean do, re, mi, fa, sol?

"Don't talk, sing."

"Will you tape it?" asked Mlakar.

The cameraman pointed his camera in Mlakar's face. And Jože Mlakar began to sing: "Do, re, mi, fa, sol, la, ti, do." People gathered around and began to laugh uproariously, especially when he sang the scale backward.

Before he disappeared, he tried once more to get onstage to speak during Independence Day celebrations, but some guards grabbed him even before he had begun to get out of his third-row seat, a seat he had gotten with a forged ticket.

The last two people to see Jože Mlakar before his disappearance were the sales clerk at the Mercator store and her boss. Neither one of them recognized him, although they certainly could have. After all, not so long ago he had been on television almost every evening. His face was a little scruffy, though not in the way that is now fashionable for men. "He seemed like a man who hadn't shaved for a while, and he hadn't changed his shirt," said the cashier, who knew about these sorts of things, given that she has to deal with all sorts of people. And the security camera had also elongated his face. Still, she should have recognized him. Ah, if only human memory were not so short; today everyone recognizes and admires you, and tomorrow no one pays attention. But the two of them had paid attention to him, particularly because he'd behaved strangely. He stood in front of the dairy case, looked into the security camera, and spoke. If she'd known it was Jože Mlakar, she would have known what he was talking about, and her manager wouldn't have had to say, "Too bad there's no sound. I'll have to go out there to hear what he's going on about."

It is likely that Jože Mlakar was speaking about human rights for the last time, but this can't be confirmed because the camera did not record sound, and by the time the manager reached the refrigerator case in the corner, he couldn't hear anything because the man was no longer there. He disappeared. His family issued a missing-person report, and for a while everyone was sure he would appear sooner or later. For a while he roamed the country, and sometimes he would call up on the phone. It seemed he would probably spend the rest of his life in search of that magic eye that would not release him from its embrace.

He was found in the wet autumn leaves not far from the bus station by the road that leads into the capital. He was lying on his back with wide-open dead eyes that were looking up into the crowns of some trees. The detectives could tell without difficulty that his killer had dragged the body from the road into the forest some thirty yards away. You could tell because the clothes and face of the dead man were all wet, and his pockets were filled with sand and leaves that could have been picked up only while he was being dragged. His wallet had fallen from his pocket along the way and, because it was empty, robbery was suspected. But this theory was shaken that same day when the desk clerk of a nearby hotel told them that the dead man had come in the previous evening to pay his long-overdue bill for a hotel room. He had wanted to pay interest as well, but the clerk had taken pity on him because of his sunken face and wouldn't take it. And in any case he couldn't have paid interest because, as the clerk could plainly see, after paying the bill there was absolutely nothing left in his wallet. Maybe he had money in his briefcase. But the briefcase, which lay in the forest not far from the body, was clearly untouched and was filled with papers written in a completely illegible hand. Because the fatal blow had been to the head and had cracked the skull, the forensic experts could tell that it had been struck by an enormous and correspondingly powerful man. And while they were walking around the corpse, taking pictures of it with their police cameras equipped with flash and reflectors, they couldn't get over his dead eyes, which looked at them malevolently, as if they were still alive, as if in the crowns of the trees they could see the enormous man who had killed him, or as if they were focused on the smooth and dark liquid surface of a deep tarn from which they could not wrench themselves away.

■ □ ■ □ ■

THE SPECTER FROM ROVENSKA

I

"What an amazing pier," she says.

"It's not a pier," he says. "It's a breakwater."

"It's amazing all the same," she says.

The air quivers in the rays of spring sunshine; the calm surface of the sea stretches between the island and the mainland. The surface reflects everything up to the mountains, whose peaks are still covered with snow. The solitary pair is standing at the far edge of a stone tongue that creeps out into the sea. Behind them lies a green island, its houses crowding against its shore. Next to them lie upturned boats, like gigantic motionless fish that were thrown ashore during the winter and are now stuck fast.

"What's so amazing?" he says. "All breakwaters are like this."

"They aren't," she says. "There's nothing to tie up to."

Indeed. Absent are those dark and rounded iron bollards, wider at the top, site of all the action when boats tie up, where agile men move with dignified gestures as they tie the hulls of their boats to the pier with heavy ropes.

"True, there are no bollards," he says, "because it's a breakwater, not a pier."

"Anyway, the sea is really shallow here," she says. "Big boats couldn't come in."

"You're right," he says. "It's really curious. Big boats clearly don't dock here."

But it's more beautiful than curious. Lošinj is green in the spring, and the sea is blue. If you're lucky you can sometimes see a pod of dolphins swimming across the shiny surface of the water. So that is why the strollers stop worrying about the amazing and obviously useless structure and instead gaze out dreamily over the surrounding scenery that God has organized so beautifully and intelligently.

2

In the midst of his verbose oration on the occasion of laying the cornerstone of the breakwater for the big port in Rovenska on the island of Lošinj in the spring of 1856, the young Austrian archduke Ferdinand Max had gazed overlong and somewhat dreamily at the shiny surface of the sea. God's intelligently ordered world was tranquil, though in the distance he saw some large fish that moved over the surface of the water, floating for a moment in the air before disappearing again beneath the surface. That sight caused him to lose the thread of his celebratory speech. He tore his gaze from the sea and turned to the crowd, which had been following his speech carefully, to continue from the point when the flying fish had interrupted him, precisely when he had reached the part about greatness.

Just then, instead of the adjutant who should have been nearby, and instead of the local bishop who was also supposed to be close at hand, he saw before him a completely impossible, somehow unnatural specter. For a moment he forgot where he was, here or somewhere else. Was he dreaming or was he really on a podium in some place whose name he had momentarily forgotten?

In front of him stood a man with an enormous head, a truly powerful head that swayed on a thin neck in a tightly buttoned collar. The man's hollow, sunken eyes gazed at him with doglike devotion, and he was holding something out in front of him. Ferdinand Max shivered. His glance strayed out to the dolphins that had again broken the surface of the water. Of course, members of the ruling family don't always think about doglike devotion but rather about assassinations, especially when a kind of specter holding some weapon in his hands is standing before them. "The mighty . . ." he tried to continue the speech, "the mighty port of a great empire . . ." But hadn't he been speaking about an outlet to the world's seas when he saw those fish and began to think, *Are those really dolphins? And who is this? What is this macrocephalous creature in front of me?* For a moment he became completely confused, for a moment he forgot where he was, on a boat, at Miramare, or somewhere else. "The mighty," he said, "the mighty port of a great empire . . . mighty." Then he suddenly saved himself by turning to words he had used happily and frequently. "By God's Providence," he said, "and by the call of fate that has chosen us . . . for . . . to accomplish great deeds."

The Lošinj captains in the first row began to applaud, music played, sailors threw their caps in the air, fishermen and peasants pushed their way into the front rows.

"The cornerstone," said the adjutant, who had noticed that the archduke had blanked out for a fairly long time. "God bless," said the bishop, who had now come up to the podium beside him. But the archduke could not tear his gaze from that enormous head, with sideburns even broader and bushier than his own.

"Who is that?" he asked nervously. "What is that?"

"It's the master mason," said his adjutant. "He's going to help set it."

"Set what?"

"The cornerstone."

"Oh, of course," said the commander of the Austrian naval forces as he shook his head sulkily: *what a head.*

3

The breakwater on which the springtime couple is walking is a monumental structure. It is two hundred yards long and the sea around it is two fathoms deep. Enormous stones from the coast near Trieste were brought in to build it. For seven years you could hear the cries of workers from all over the empire, the blows of stonecutters' hammers, and the slicing of saws. Some lost their lives here, and they left their foreign names in the cemetery up above it. The beauty of the area leads the pair to ask new questions about the meaning of this human endeavor. In the background, on the mainland, are snowcapped mountains, the sea glistens, the good sun and pleasant moon light up the breakwater and the cemetery—all this mighty meaninglessness. Their intuition tells them that this enormous creation of human hands is in amazing disharmony with the beautiful and intelligent order of God's creation all around. That is correct. In fact the breakwater serves no real purpose. No ship works or port was ever built, and because there are not even any bollards, no ships ever tied up to the breakwater. What remains is a horizontal monument in the water, a fallen stone obelisk that lies here only to recall the pitiful and senseless fate of the person who laid its cornerstone. And of those others whose lives were caught up by that fate and who lie buried in the nearby pine forest, as well as those whose bodies have disintegrated in the damp of distant Mexican winters.

4

Archduke Ferdinand Max was in a bad mood. He'd gotten mixed up in the middle of his speech. His brother in Vienna would find out that he'd gotten mixed up in the most routine talk. And not just mixed up; in full view of a hundred pairs of eyes he'd gotten scared. He'd been scared by some bumpkin with an enormous head who'd been holding an ordinary mason's trowel in his hands. He'd been daydreaming about fish that were flying above the water like his thoughts. He'd floated with them for a moment through the air above the blue surface. And when he'd reached his apogee the big-headed specter had appeared to frighten him. It had to be admitted: he'd been frightened by his own subject. The contrast was outrageous—first the dolphins over the water, then right next to him some quiet and dark shadow, some kind of big-headed specter, narrow down below and rounded up above, with sunken, doglike, loyal eyes. He'd wanted to push this subject, who was devoted and oafish, like all his subjects, or to hit him. He had barely gotten hold of himself. During lunch he discovered that the name of this master mason, or whatever he was, was headlike in his Slovene language, like Kopf or Kurbiskopf, or something even funnier. This calmed him down and even allowed him to laugh a bit. "He really does have an amazing head," said the adjutant, "though he is the best worker. That's why he was given the honor of helping to lay the cornerstone."

After lunch he asked for him to be called over, so that he could again see the creature who had interfered with his thoughts as they flew high over the water's surface.

5

"What is your name, young man?"

"Glavan," said the builder, who was not really young, older than the archduke in any case, "my name is Ivan Glavan."

"Glavan," said Ferdinand Max.

"It means *Kopf* in German, a big one."

"Amazing," said the archduke.

Glavan explained that there was nothing amazing about it. In his Slovene village Glavine, practically everyone had that name. One of the Lošinj captains added that around here they called people with big heads *glavonja. We call them Wasserkopf,* thought the archduke, and he smiled. He discovered that the young Slovene peasant had worked in a quarry on the coast. There he had become a master mason. The archduke knew about that quarry, for that was where the stones had been cut for Miramare Castle. Ivan Glavan from Glavine in Slovenia knew Miramare well; he'd made the fountain in the park. The archduke now warmed to him and slowly even got used to the unpleasant sight of the enormous head, and even to the sideburns, which, like his own, unfortunately reminded him of his brother. Soon he was completely at ease. Again he looked out at the sea's surface through the gardens. The enormous fish that had jumped out of the water during his speech were a good omen; now he felt sure of that. And as for that big-headed fellow whom he had taken to be a bad omen because he had scared him for no reason at all, now he saw that he was actually a pleasant subject, who made fountains and built breakwaters. He ordered Glavan, "How do you say it? . . . Glavankopf, yes, get Glavankopf a glass of wine. And when he had toasted the best worker, he said a few words that would change the life of the young master mason. He said, "Keep it up, Glavankopf, just keep it up."

6

When, several years later, amid the Mexican mountains of the Sierra Madre, Ivan Glavan would describe in a moving voice what had happened to him on a far-off southern island of the empire, those historic words would still be ringing in his ears. His martial comrades gathered around the campfire would look at his enormous head with great respect, and that same head would be recalled with fear and respect across the Mexican plateaus. They would know that the eyes of this terrifying warrior fill with tears whenever he talks about a breakwater on an Adriatic island, and that his powerful head falls forward onto his chest at this memory. Here in the Mexican mountains Ivan Glavan would still hear the words that changed his life. He would still see the archduke's plumed hat waving above the heads of the Lošinj captains and their wives, above the bishops and the merchants, above the fishermen and peasants, even above the Lošinj pines and cypresses, even above the church's campanile when seen from a Mexican perspective. And, ah, high above everything he would see the snowcapped mountains of his homeland in his mind's eye. Ivan Glavan would never experience anything more beautiful than that spring day on Lošinj.

He was in seventh heaven, as they say. It was the high point of his life. He had helped to lay the cornerstone of an enormous port of an enormous empire. The archduke, who would perhaps one day be the emperor, had said to him, "Keep it up, Ivan Glavankopf." All the stonecutters in the quarry, all his fellow villagers from Glavine in Slovenia, his father, mother, sister, brother, they would all have nodded their enormous, self-satisfied, and proud heads, they would have all said, "That's our Ivan."

It was an event that would stay with him until his final hours. In Ferdinand Max's eyes, seen from up close, he had glimpsed the goodness and decisiveness that can be found only in the eyes of rulers destined for great deeds. After all, right in front of him, to him in fact, he had also said: "By God's Providence," he had said, "and by the call of fate that has chosen us . . . for." Here the future emperor had deliberately added a pause that gave his words even more effect: "to accomplish great deeds." He'd looked at the sea for a long time before he had said those words, and he said them to the sea and to him. And then Ivan Glavan had looked with emotion at the plume, which had waved with great dignity over all the other heads and swooped like an enormous bird that was about to fly up into the air, circle the island and the sea, and fly off toward the snowcapped mountains.

Then and there he swore, as he recounted many years later in the Sierra Madres, to help that man accomplish the great deeds to which he was called, to serve him to the grave.

7

The celebration of the laying of the cornerstone for the breakwater in Rovenska was over. For a time Ferdinand Max continued to think about the man who had been standing in front of him when he'd turned away from the sea. He'd observed dolphins leaping from the water, and because it was well known that he liked to dream, it hadn't been difficult to compare the fish leaping through the air with his own high-flying thoughts and desires, which he would have to rein in some day. But he had not been called into this world and into this ruling house in order, from his twentieth birthday on, to go to ceremonies and launch projects like hospitals, theaters, or ports. He was convinced, as was well known, that fate held more important things in store for him than laying cornerstones for the construction of breakwaters. Indeed, for a moment he'd recognized that fact in all its clarity in those shining fish that had flown like shimmering specters above the water, above the sea's gleaming surface. *That,* he thought, *is how one should fly, like those fish . . . They fly,* he thought for an instant, *although they live in the water.* This thought flashed suddenly through him, and for a moment it made him somewhat dizzy. Later he thought about that moment quite frequently, for it had probably changed his life. And he could not understand it in any other way than as a message that no life is completely given, that it can be transformed into a higher form. If fish are called out of the water into the air toward the sun, then he too could be chosen for great deeds. Whenever he would call this scene to mind in later years, he could never repeat it without recalling the feeling of unease, the inchoate fear that had followed, and the anger at himself because of the annoying person who had been standing under his very nose just at the moment when he had been seized by great insight and when he had wanted to conclude his speech effectively. Even though he had eventually calmed down and they had drunk to each other's health, he couldn't banish the thought that he had become confused because he had truly been scared by that what's-his-name? . . . Kurbis . . . or Wasserkopf?

In time he thought less frequently about the dolphins that had floated above the water and about the big-headed shade that had stood by him. History approached with big strides, and it was time for the most important decisions in his life. And that was why he also stopped worrying about the construction of the enormous breakwater for the even more enormous harbor in Rovenska. Great deeds had arrived for him to accomplish, those things he had always known would come, those things that fate had predicted and that would finally catch up to him and thrust him out of the water into the sunlight.

8

Ivan Glavan worked winter and summer. He walked amid the stones, giving orders, helping pull the winches, adjusting the stonecutting saws, under the broiling summer sun and in the cold snow flurries that winter storms blew into his face. The breakwater grew slowly. The sea was voracious, and they had to pile, push, and shove enormous quantities of stone into it. Brigantines and little lighters sank under the weight of enormous pieces of stone that were shipped from quarries up the coast. Oxen bellowed, and under the weight of the stones from the Lošinj quarries the wheels of carts cracked on the dusty roads, the craggy banks, and the gravel. Sometimes Glavan thought they were building something as enormous as the Egyptian pyramids illustrated in one of his technical books. And it felt good to be part of such a feat of labor. When he was alone, he would listen to the south winds that wafted in heat from the sea, to the cicadas, and to the sea rolling against the shore. He would think that he should put his life in order, perhaps travel back to his home in the Slovene mountains or up the coast where he had worked in the quarries and bring back a wife. But somehow he knew that his life was marked out for something different, for some kind of greater endeavor. If he had suspected this before, he had become absolutely sure of it after his meeting with archduke Ferdinand Max. His sideburns already looked like the emperor's and the archduke's, but now he decided to comb his hair and beard down the middle in accordance with contemporary Viennese fashion, exaggerated à la Ferdinand Max. All he achieved was that, whereas before he had been laughed at only for his enormous head, now he was also mocked for his bushy sideburns and the way he parted his hair and beard. He was a sweet man, though he had a quick temper. He didn't mind jokes about his head, even in his own village where, because everyone had a head like that, they liked to mock one another. But he could not stand anyone laughing at the cut of his hair and beard, which was done out of respect for the imperial house and as a sign of devotion to the great man who had said, "Keep it up, Glavankopf." That was why, when a Hungarian worker had laughed at the imperial part of his hair and beard in a restaurant one day, Ivan suddenly pulled out a tuft of his hair. He pressed him between his knees with a spadelike hand, grabbed him by his black curls, and jerked his head. Instead of hair the mocker found himself with a bloody scalp. Glavan had to laugh. "Now the kid's hair is parted properly," he said, "an imperial part."

In comparison to everything else that Ivan Glavan would do for the ruler toward whom he felt such attachment, that incident in a Lošinj tavern is hardly noteworthy. It is worth mentioning because similar actions would produce legendary stories about a man whose name would be pronounced with fear and respect in the cities, on the mountain roads, and in the desert plains of a far-off land. It would be pronounced in another language—they would call him Cabezón, which means something like "big head." It also refers to a stubborn and dangerous man who is ready for anything and whom one should not cross.

9

As far as Ferdinand Max was concerned, for some time nothing pushed him toward higher things, toward the fate that had been predicted for him by the flying fish near the place called Rovenska. They had ascended from the thick and gooey world of substance into the airy heights, effortlessly freed from gravity, but he could not do it. Slowly he began to doubt whether he would ever step out of the shadow of his great brother, who ruled the empire with a mighty hand. From Miramare Castle he gazed gloomily at the rainy autumn evenings. It is said that one morning he used his hands and teeth to rip up an invitation to dedicate a hospital with an insane asylum near

Ljubljana. "No more cornerstones," he cried, "no more hospitals, no more accursed theaters."

Nevertheless, Lady Fate approached. But when she arrived, he was depressed and full of doubt. The business of the Mexican throne that had been hanging in the air for years already, and about which he had almost given up hope, budged again. Ferdinand Max was asked to become emperor of Mexico at the invitation of the Mexican grandees who wanted neither a republic nor its President Juárez, and thanks to the persuasion of the French court, whose expeditionary forces had gotten France firmly entangled in Mexican affairs.

The tangle of fates that would suck him into the whirlpool finally appeared, and in an instant the plan charmed the thirty-year-old archduke. There were plenty of warnings: Juárez's republicans, despite the defeat the French expeditionary forces had inflicted on them, were still powerful, so it would not be a simple triumphal march but a real war. Mexico was far away, and the future was by no means clear. His sober imperial brother in Vienna tried to deflect him from this romantic giddiness with a combination of persuasion and threats. *Mexico is not Miramare. There you will find another sky, another land, different people and animals.* But the young archduke knew—the call of fate comes only once. You have to answer it and conquer the earth's gravity to fly up into the heights. His beautiful wife, the Belgian princess Charlotte, saw in the offer that same Providence about which Max had spoken of so frequently, and she embraced the Mexican plan with gusto.

On April 8, 1864, archduke Ferdinand Max renounced his dynastic rights in Austria. His imperial brother had agreed that he could call for volunteers. The Mexican crown was brought to Miramare Castle on April 9, and on June 18, with the help of the French expeditionary forces, he marched solemnly into the capital city of Mexico. He had made up his mind, taken the risk, and ascended where the call of fate led. He would remain Maximilian, emperor of Mexico, to the end. And the end was not far off.

10

The construction of the breakwater in Rovenska proceeded, as it is said, at a crawl, and regarding the beginning of construction of the enormous port and ship works there was not a sound to be heard. It was said, however, that the ship works would be built in the town of Little Lošinj because it was better situated. One evening in the garden of the villa belonging to a ship captain with whom he had been drinking, Ivan Glavan heard an incredible moaning and sobbing, an incoherent speech about a horrible mistake that could never be fixed. This was one of the Lošinj captains who had invested his entire fortune in the Rovenska breakwater. He blundered about the garden as if seasick, sprinkled his conversation with incomprehensible Italian words, and finally threw up over the fence as though there were a billowing sea on the other side. Glavan was amazed, and many thoughts arose in his enormous head, chasing after one another inside that enormous space. He could not understand how it was possible that the construction of such a great thing as his great lord had thought up could just stop. But ever less money flowed in to build the breakwater, and the workers began to leave. It became impossible to find men to work in the quarry. Ever more frequently the captains and boat owners walked around the half-built breakwater and waved their hands furiously. Whenever anyone would approach, they would quiet down. It was strange. Nor was the master mason Glavan worthy of their confidence, for when they saw him approaching in the distance they would quickly shut up. Ivan Glavan believed you should finish what you start. And so he would have stayed at the breakwater until his dying day. Those are the kind of people who come from his Slovene village; in addition to having big heads, they are unusually tenacious, quick to anger, and stubborn.

One evening Ivan Glavan read an article in the newspaper that made his heart race. Ferdinand Max had become the emperor of Mexico. The Mexican emperor Maximilian was recruiting volunteers to help him tame the stubborn Mexicans who dared contest his rule. His heart didn't merely race; it began to beat like a heavy hammer at a quarry. He knew he couldn't delay for an instant. Of course, it was too bad he would not be able to see the completion of the breakwater that he, who by God's grace and the call of fate was now the emperor of Mexico, had begun to build. But he heard the same call of fate that had found Ferdinand Max in Miramare. He knew he had to help, and he roared over the sea like a wolf. The hammer beat in his chest, and inside his cranial space his own lupine howl echoed, "I'm coming, king. Ivan is coming to help."

He heard what Ferdinand Max told him: "Keep it up, Glavankopf, just keep it up."

II

And just when the emperor, shining with glory, at the apogee of his life, was riding into the capital of Mexico in the company of his generals to the sounds of trumpets and drums, a middle-aged man who attracted widespread attention was standing by the entrance to a former sugar mill in Ljubljana. The scene by the entrance was always bustling, for under an enormous red and white flag emblazoned with the word *Mexico* crowded groups of young men who had signed up for the Mexican expedition. And when, amid the "Mexicanos," as the Slovenes called the volunteers, there appeared a man with a head large enough for three and imperial sideburns that evoked respect, the windows of the building filled with curious onlookers who had nothing to do but be curious. "The emperor," someone called out, "the emperor has arrived." Laughter rang out in the corridors and the courtyard.

"This one will scare them," said the recruitment officer, who also wanted to laugh and who could not tear his eyes from Glavan's head.

"And also serve for target practice," someone else said.

Glavan said nothing. He took his ten gold coins and sent the money to his village. He needed nothing more than bread and his kit. Glavan was not going overseas for the money. Many of the Slovene volunteers were going for the wealth they thought was there for the taking or for the dark-skinned girls who were waiting for the same thing. Ivan Glavan knew why he was going. For the inscription embroidered on a cloth in every house in the village of Glavine—"for faith, fatherland, and emperor." Even though the word *fatherland* did sound a bit unnatural when applied to the wild and distant Mexican territories, he knew that this had all been imprinted on the hearts and in the big heads of his ancestors. In the evening he listened to the song the young men were singing on the banks of the Ljubljanica River:

"We are fine guys,
Mexicanos.
We're going to fight
Out there in Mexico."

And his big head fell to his chest. And when he heard the continuation,

"Emperor Maximilian
He's been chosen
To rule
And sent to Mexico . . ."

two tears fell from the deep wells of his eye sockets and rolled down his long cheeks. It was as if the song said exactly what he was feeling in his heart. The emperor was alone in Mexico, surrounded by hostile forces. Ivan Glavan was strong and strong willed, loyal and powerful. What had to happen had happened, what he had long been waiting for, ever since the moment when the emperor had spoken his great words to him—it always seemed to him that they had been spoken to him alone—and gazed at him with his totally regal eyes.

12

And when, a month later in Trieste, he boarded the English steamer *Indiana* together with three hundred Austrian volunteers, and when in the distance he saw the island of Lošinj, he knew: those words had been directed precisely at him and at no one else—or to all who were capable of hearing the call of fate. And as they floated past Lošinj, that distant green island, he clearly heard the words that had been directed at him and the sea once more, words in all their power at the beginning of the building of a mighty port. He recalled their sound, repeated them; how many nights had they rung in his ears on Lošinj, how many days in the fields when he was returning home, those words that only now, as he was en route to Mexico, had revealed their prophetic power: "By God's Providence," said Maximilian, the emperor of Mexico, "and by the call of fate, that has chosen us . . . for . . . to accomplish great deeds."

And when the *Indiana* sailed through the Straits of Messina, he heard those words again, wafting across the water's surface, sailing with them through the straits; keep it up, just keep it up; and he heard them a few days later under the decks amid the stinking men when they reached Gibraltar, an island inhabited by black men, when he saw the famous hollow mountain fortified with eight hundred heavy cannon. And when, on the great ocean a storm blew up that lasted four days and nights, and when one of the men died and was given to the sharks, then too he knew that all of this had to be endured because he was being propelled by the cry of the lonely emperor.

They stepped onto dry land for the first time on January 8, 1865. They debarked on Martinique and spent the night in a French citadel half an hour away. There they found a French garrison. It was January, and it was warm. The French offered them some sweet fruits that were neither pears nor oranges. They had locked up some dark-skinned women in a little house close by the citadel and were collecting a fee for them. The men who went said they were cheap and beautiful. It was hot, sweet, cheap, and beautiful. Mexico was close by; all they had to do was to debark on its shores and take the place.

But Ivan Glavan did not sample the fruits, nor did he want to see the dark-skinned women.

He walked around the cathedral of St. Louis, admired the structure, the sculptures, and the many varieties of marble, and he thought of his construction, the breakwater at Rovenska that he had left unfinished. And this was fitting, because the call of his ruler's fate had appealed to him to make something new of his own life. He sat on a bench in the church, looked at the shining stained-glass rose window, and prayed not for himself but for Emperor Maximilian. He was now quite close to his emperor.

They embarked the very next day; they needed to hurry, for the Mexican emperor Maximilian was eagerly awaiting his Austrians who were to accomplish great deeds.

13

It really was time to accomplish them, because soon after his glorious entrance into the capital city things had gotten difficult for Emperor Maximilian. In fact, to tell the truth, he was really hard pressed. It wasn't just that the French suddenly showed a complete lack of interest in fighting. He was beset by a number of plots organized not only by Juárez, that able and decisive son of Mexican peasants, but also by a cabal of European courts and American diplomats. He suddenly realized that his power was built on shaky foundations. The landowners who had come to fetch him from Miramare disappeared, and nothing remained of the solemn entry. Once, when he was standing by the window in the middle of the hot night, some mestizo called out to him from the courtyard and disappeared. He recognized the man as one of the stable boys. When he asked what the man had said, there was hesitation. Some women laughed loudly when he passed by. He gave an order to find the man. His soldiers searched the entire palace and all the stables, but the man had simply melted away. Two days later he heard the same cry, and laughter again, this time from the street. Now he knew what was so funny. The cry meant, "You came for your funeral."

The thought came to him that he should give up, right now at the beginning. He found himself in a land he did not understand and did not love. As opposed to Miramare, where the peasants looked at him with doglike devotion or at least with oafish glances, here they cried out that he had come for his own funeral and God knows what other stupidities. Juárez and his republican forces were in control of a good portion of the country, it was hot, no one knew how to chill wine properly, instead of porcelain they had some kind of crockery—fate's call was suddenly unpleasant, humid, and hot. Nothing was glorious anymore; the whole thing had become arduous and perhaps dangerous.

Most of all it appeared that God's Providence, to which he had so happily appealed and which had, in addition to himself, attracted thousands of young people to this distant country, did not have any plan for the great deeds that Maximilian had spoken about to Glavankopf and to the sea. There were only political intrigues, humidity, rain, mud, wild animals, death, illness, and his decorous wife who would be driven insane by this disturbing world. In a word, in the plan was agony, and it followed inevitably.

14

God's Providence had, perhaps, prepared an even more terrible denouement for those thousands who followed him expecting to be new conquistadores on the road to a land of easier martial triumph—triumphant rides through conquered cities and riches—than had been provided for the conquest some centuries earlier. It would include wolfish war cries, the bloody stumps of amputated limbs, waterside insects, women raped by both armies, yellow fever in prison camps, flies that live in the sand and burrow into the skin, particularly into wounds, and that have to be dug out.

On the *Indiana,* transporting the Slovene volunteers to help their emperor, no one knows anything about this.

The oceanic storms are behind them, and they are approaching the warm shores of triumph, of victorious marches through villages and towns, and as they arrive in the town of Vera Cruz this song can be heard on the deck:

"Emperor Maximilian,
He's been chosen
To rule
And sent to Mexico."

On February 2 they docked at the port of Vera Cruz, where all fates flowed together, of those arriving and departing, of the living and the dead. It would be from this very port, a few years later, that Admiral Tegetthoff would collect the beaten and destroyed army on board the ship *Novara,* and the Mexicanos would be together with the corpse of their emperor. As pathetic as that departure would be, so the arrival was sinister: along all the streets and squares waddled quite friendly vultures who dealt with the carrion, which was always in sufficient supply.

Here they were and they had to go on.

15

Glavan was assigned to a company of scouts, and the scouts always started off first; to Orizaba, then to Oaxaca, and on to the high Sierra Madre range. At Orizaba God gave them a victory, and the boys said that this was their Sisek. Just as once upon a time Slovene forces had defeated the Turks at Sisek, so at Orizaba in Mexico, a little detachment of fifty Slovene soldiers defeated a much larger group of *los chicanos,* as they laughingly called those who belonged to the anti-imperial forces. And what were *los chicanos* if not Turks? Three members of Glavan's detachment were killed, and two soldiers were wounded. The enemy left eighteen dead and seventy-three wounded soldiers on the battlefield. As Ivan Glavan would recount much later, the tigers, hyenas, and vultures could thank his group for their first meal. There are no tigers in Mexico. Glavan had probably seen jaguars or some other cats devoting themselves to their prey. In that battle they acquired so many horses and mules that the infantry became a cavalry.

Here Ivan Glavan killed his first enemy. He was one of *los chicanos,* thus an infidel, a republican, a liberal, some kind of Turk, but even so he cried out horribly when the bayonet slid through the torn shirt, through the thin skin, into the little stomach of that little man whose ribs stuck out through his skin. He screamed horribly, as if he really had a soul that was departing somewhere. When bloody sweat oozed through the bronze skin of the prone man, he pulled himself up on his elbow and called on the Virgin of Guadalupe. That's like the Mother of God from Ptujska Gora, explained his friend Juretz, who knew all about Mexico and how to die there. "He's not a heathen," said Glavan, and he leaned his enormous head down sadly over the small, dying man. "He's whispering something," he said, and Juretz also leaned down.

"Despierta, mi alma, despierta," whispered the small, dying foe.

"What's he saying?" asked Glavan.

" 'Awake, my soul, awake,' he's saying," said Juretz.

Then he gasped again, and his soul departed. It would never wake again. Glavan's enormous head suddenly became empty, and something tightened in his throat. *I killed a man,* he thought. *I've never killed a man before.* And a tear might have fallen down his large face had he not heard in that empty cranial space a voice he knew so well: "Just keep it up, Glavankopf, keep it up."

He stood up, looked at Juretz, and said, "Did you hear that?"

"No," said Juretz, "what?"

"A voice," said Glavan.

"What voice?"

"A voice said, 'Just keep it up.' "

"That's how it is," said Juretz, "when you kill your first one. At first it causes a bit of a disturbance in your head. Then it's OK."

Undoubtedly the victory in this small skirmish was just the beginning. And in Oaxaca, when they gazed with awe at an enormous tree so big it took thirty of them to encircle it, that was also just the beginning. And when they were attacked by two thousand cavalrymen near Decomobaca and formed a *carré* and fired all night long until toward morning the cavalrymen melted off into the mountains, that was also just the beginning. Only when they got to the high Sierra Madre and began to be attacked at every step, and when their mules together with their guides fell headlong into the abyss, did they finally understand that they had gotten to a place from which there was probably no return because this, as the Mexicanos sang, was a completely different world.

16

While Glavan pressed forward on one side of the country, his emperor was retreating on the other. Emperor Maximilian quickly left the capital together with a powerful army as soon as Juárez's forces came dangerously close. At some estate, a resting place was arranged, a poor, temporary capital. He would only be here for a couple of days, Colonel López reassured him. Then they would return triumphantly to the capital. But the days turned into weeks and the weeks into months. Then the rains came. Every day there was warm, slimy rain that soaked everything, the earth and the plants, and carried mud into the dining rooms and the bedrooms. Souls were soaked and faces darkened. Maximilian walked around morosely, drank more than necessary, and worst of all, he dabbed a handkerchief dipped in eau de cologne on his nose all day long. On the advice of one of the monarchists who had come to Miramare to offer him the Mexican throne—a throne, not this mud and dirt—he had become convinced that eau de cologne mixed liberally with wine was the best defense against the yellow fever that had begun to rage all around. He placed great stock in this advice and in the monarchists' offer right up until his, not their, death.

One night, amid the noise of the rain, in a hopeless timelessness, in an atmosphere permeated by humidity, eau de cologne, and wine, Maximilian agreed that Charlotte should return to Europe. Charlotte was a courageous woman. She was constantly exhorting Maximilian to honorable perseverance. She usually drove away his backsliding and hesitation, but that evening, when she saw Max's gray face in that handkerchief dipped in eau de cologne, she came to a decision. She would set off for Europe; she would get the European monarchs to help him. They would send an expeditionary force to help Maximilian; the pope would give his blessing.

17

Not long after his arrival in Vera Cruz, Glavan acquired a reputation that spread through all parts of Mexico wherever Austrian soldiers went, and among the Indians and mestizos who spoke with great respect about the terrifying Austrian with the enormous head.

As he was happy to recount later, it was an agreeable happenstance. It all began in some *pulquería* where they served an alcoholic drink made from cactus juice. And when at about ten o'clock he came out of the *pulquería,* full of that alcoholic drink, he was attacked by two men armed with swords. Glavan, however, was full not only of pulque but also of courage and martial faith. And those two men, as he would recount later, did not know how to handle their deadly weapons nearly as well as he his cutlass. "Keep it up, guys," he said, "just keep it up." In three minutes both of the men were lying on the ground with their heads split from their jaws to their temples. Because one of the attackers had been the gang leader Don Pancho de Boca, whom everyone feared, his glory now belonged to the even more terrifying Glavan.

That very morning he got his name, the enormous-headed name Cabezón, which in years to come would be spoken with respect around many campfires by Austrian forces and European adventurers, as well as by the republicans.

Among the Indians this white man with a head big enough for three acquired a reputation as terrifying as that of the former Spanish conquerors. His monumental head, with its imposing sideburns, with the part in the hair and the beard, was frequently taken for a specter: devilish, divine, imperial, or butcherlike. Upon hearing that Cabezón was coming, a whole troop of mestizos was seized with terrified panic; soldiers jumped out of windows. Children ran out of the streets whenever he appeared, and some songs dating from the time of that unhappy expedition speak about his enormous head and call him the scourge of God. There was nothing unnatural about his having a big head, for God can be terrifying in Mexico. In fact, he is known for that there. Ivan Glavan did not care about his reputation. He shot, hacked at human flesh, used his bayonet and rifle butt, and did his duty just as he had done while building the breakwater in Rovenska, in heat or cold, when the wild winds blew, and on humid nights. And with each shot, with each cut or blow he heard the emperor's words: "Just keep it up, Glavankopf, just keep it up."

18

The emperor was melancholy: Charlotte had sailed away; the nightingales had died. Around Maximilian everything began to take on the contours of fate once again. But this time there were no fish leaping from the depths of the sea into the sunlight. There were nightingales, dying in the cages of their fate.

When he was in the capital with the sun streaming down, he had wanted to hear the singing of nightingales from the Karst or at least from the aviaries of Miramare Castle. And the next naval vessel to arrive from across the ocean ferried four hundred new volunteers and three hundred nightingales. Some, volunteers and nightingales, had died in the course of the choppy passage across the ocean. The rest arrived in Mexico alive.

This was a great comfort to him, for Charlotte had finally really departed after a long delay. As with everything else in this country, her voyage had turned into a nightmare. It was said that in Puebla, where they were spending the night, she woke up the servants in the middle of the night and in their company went into the empty house of the king's former prefect. At her request the house was unlocked and she ran through the empty rooms all night long. In Vera Cruz she had demanded that the French flag be removed from the boat. When she arrived in Europe and met with Napoleon III, visitors to the park of St.-Cloud heard a piercing cry: "Sire, you have allowed me to be poisoned." In the Vatican she fell to the feet of Pope Pius IX and asked him to protect her and her husband from murderers. Many years later a researcher would claim that her strange behavior was caused by poison. The poison of a Mexican mushroom that is called *teyhuinti,* a poison that causes a special kind of insanity, first contentiousness, then a state of harmless idiocy, *mens insana in corpore sano.*

She traveled in the direction of her insanity, under the care of Dr. Samuel Basch, traveled to the empty rooms of Miramare, and then to her empty Belgian castle, traveled into trashy novels, which would use her melancholy fate in tearjerker plots for the next hundred years—and with the hint that she had departed pregnant by one of Maximilian's commanders, with the hint that she had departed because Maximilian had gotten involved with some Indian woman and adopted her child. In any case, Charlotte had departed and Maximilian had only nightingales.

But now the sun was no longer shining anywhere in Mexico, there were no more royal palaces and gardens, and no more light. There was some kind of hacienda in a muddy plateau, it poured rain every day, and it was cold and wet.

He listened to their singing with closed eyes and recognized grimly that there was less and less of it, that these lively birds were withering in their wet cages, just as his own dark and unhappy soul was withering in the winter in this wet and cold country.

Then the nightingales began to die. One after another they died; their little corpses shook in the emperor's horrified hands. Maximilian ran from cage to cage, pouring them water and giving them sunflower seeds, pumpkin seeds, and all sorts of bird treats, seeds, crumbs, and grasses. He called the doctors from the nearest military hospital, but nothing could be done.

It was as if in this horrible dying he saw another metaphor of his own fate.

19

That is another world, as the Slovene Mexicanos sang, and that other world was one of carrion and vultures, of a shortage of fresh water, of foul odors, of dampness, of vermin and sudden despair: where have we come to? One Count Carmy ended his Mexican expedition as soon as it began. He jumped out of the boat in despair, and thus put an end to his suffering. In the days that followed, many succumbed to despair. Instead of a sunny land they would march through triumphantly, they found themselves burdened with swords, shovels, tents, and munitions. On forced marches through the interior of the country their aching bodies were baked by the sun. Their clothes were lousy, and they were harassed by mosquitoes and all kinds of insects. And soon afterward the enemy began to attack from all sides. *Los chicanos* were not an incompetent gang of lazy Mexicans who would run away at the first shot, but bloody and pitiless warriors who attacked from ambushes. In hand-to-hand combat they used sharp machetes, which, in the wake of their horrifying whistles through the air and their blunt cuts in human flesh, left stumps streaming blood.

Glavan knew why he was cutting into human flesh. Someone had to do this for the emperor, just as someone had to build a breakwater and carry heavy stones onto the pile. He knew that some day he would be rewarded; he hoped that the emperor would hear about him, about his difficult and courageous work, about the blows, the cuts, the bones that crunched beneath the butt of his gun. And he knew that sooner or later he would see him again from up close, and that he would look again into those big and keen eyes as he once had in the little place on the island of Lošinj in his far-off Austrian home. And then he would say—he didn't know what would be said, but certainly something memorable, something like what the emperor had said to him that sunny spring day when they had laid the cornerstone together for the powerful port of a powerful empire at the then unknown town of Rovenska. But a town that would soon be spoken of as convincingly as Trieste or Hamburg or Gdansk—and in whose chronicles would appear the name of the Mexican emperor Maximilian and his hero Ivan Glavan, also known by his Mexican name, by the glorious name that inspired fear and respect: Cabezón.

20

The emperor had heard the tales that were making the rounds about a soldier from Slovenia who was particularly courageous and exceptionally cruel to his enemies. They were especially afraid of his enormous head, which could be seen wherever the battle was fiercest and also when the soldier would order the mestizos to stand up against a wall before he would shoot them and let their bodies fall into the dust. He thought that he should thank him in some way, and that he had once seen a man with a particularly enormous head. But so great was the number of people he had met, and so enormous were the problems that beset him now, that he almost forgot about the soldier whom the mestizos called Cabezón and whom he had wanted to reward in some way. He wanted to call Colonel Miguel López, who had become his right-hand man in everything, and tell him to find that Slovene and give him some kind of medal. He had already reached for the bell when he heard the rumbling of wheels: the post had arrived.

Hungry for news from home, he forgot the courageous soldier in a moment; with trembling fingers he tore open the envelopes and greedily read through a couple of lines of letters or some pages of newspapers. His glance leapt to an article from *Die Presse* about the horrible war in Mexico. The article spoke about the cruelty of the republican armies, especially about the mestizos who knew no mercy, no limits in their blind vindictiveness for the defeats that had been inflicted on them by the brave soldiers of the legitimate Emperor Maximilian. It was unfortunate, continued *Die Presse,* that in the French and American press there were accusations of excessive cruelty committed by the Austrians, that is, by the emperor's men. Among the Austrians there were supposedly some officers and soldiers who had committed massacres in the region of Vera Cruz, and they wrote particularly about one Slovene who spread real fear and trembling among the enemy, though it was unfortunate that he had apparently lost his feeling of noblesse oblige toward the defeated. He was taken for a butcher and a slaughterer, for a specter whose deadly attacks occurred now on one, now on the other, side of the vast country. Maximilian balled the newspaper up in his hands. If that is how they were putting it in Vienna, imagine what they were writing in France and Belgium. Poor Charlotte, who had to read that. He called Colonel López, grabbed the balled-up paper, and shoved it into his face.

López's German was bad, so the emperor translated for him.

"It's possible," López said, "but after all there's a war on here."

"I want this investigated," said the emperor.

"There's nothing to investigate," said López, "since the massacre was carried out by that Slovene whom the Indians call the butcher. The emperor's butcher," he added.

"Sanctioned with no mercy," said the emperor.

"You have to remember," said López, "what the faithful warrior understands—a tooth for a tooth."

"Immediately," said the emperor.

"They run away from him," López said. He has an enormous head, and they take him for a specter. In our position . . ."

"In our position," said the emperor, "we shoot republicans because they are republicans. And we will shoot any of our soldiers who are worse than they are."

"If your honor wouldn't take offense, I'd remind you that this is the same soldier whom you wanted to—" said López.

"To execute," said the emperor. "Find him and execute him," he said. "The butcher. Do you understand?"

Colonel López understood.

Emperor Maximilian walked to the window. He could see Vienna, and he could see someone dipping his roll in a cup of coffee with milk in a downtown café, an open newspaper in front of him.

"*Die Presse,*" he said. "Yes, that's right: execute him."

21

Cabezón and Juretz were happy because they had shot a deer whose scientific name is *Dama vulgaris.* They'd shot it and butchered it, and the men had roasted its meat all night long.

Then they marched through a hollow called Las Bocas de Acatlán.

They continued on from there that very day, and on August 18 they engaged the enemy near the Río Salado. An army of fifteen hundred men under the command of the liberal general Figuera attacked them from two sides. Bloodied men and horses of both sides fell in the cross fire. Major Klein, in command of the Austrian scouts, sent a group of twenty poor uhlans against eight hundred cavalrymen. Eleven of them fell. An hour later, under strong pressure, the scouts arranged themselves in fighting order. Exhausted, hungry, and thirsty, they leapt upon the enemy and with enormous effort managed to occupy a rocky slope that was the key to the whole position. There were dead men all around, as well as groaning and wounded men and boys who could no longer be helped. Only fourteen healthy men remained. Glavan, with his imperial sideburns, his mustache and hair mussed instead of parted down the middle, was there with his majestic head that floated above everyone else like a flag, a martial banner of the battling empire; he roared, shoved, attacked, and successfully avoided blows. "Just keep it up, Glavankopf," he cried, "for faith, for fatherland, and for the emperor." Bullets whizzed around his head, and it was incredible, almost miraculous, that neither in that battle nor in any future battle did a single bullet hit his enormous head. For it made, as the officer in Ljubljana had once said, an excellent target.

Many had fallen, Major Klein among them, and now they were being led by Corporal Gönhy. They occupied an excellent position, and their slope could be defended against a much stronger force. They fired whenever they could, and no shot was wasted. Whenever the enemy came close, it was not difficult to send them, one after another, over the cliff. It went on that way all night long. But by morning they had expended all their ammunition, and nothing remained but to surrender.

It was not easy to decide to surrender, however. Terrible stories about the cruelty of *los chicanos* were going around. They left the bloody wounded to the wild beasts, the tigers, the hyenas, and the vultures. They roasted people on fires and cut off their legs and ears. They hung them over anthills, where large quantities of enormous ants slowly began with the soft parts of the body: eyes, tongue, brains, and innards. A man would live longer than necessary, and in the end there would be a skeleton hanging on a tree. Despite this, it did not occur to anyone to take his own life. The times were not heroic, and the hill that had been protecting them had no name.

So Corporal Gönhy took off his blood-soaked shirt, stuck it on the end of his bayonet, and announced their surrender.

Never again, thought Glavan, *never again will I see my beloved Emperor Maximilian. His call brought me to this land, but I will not be able to walk with him through the divine city of Puebla, and then under triumphal arches into Mexico City, and through the city to the emperor's palace amid flowers and the sounds of Austrian marches all the way to the decorated port in Trieste, to the triumphal arches in Ljubljana and the enthusiastic cries in Vienna.* They would have walked in parallel, as they had walked in parallel up until now, side by side, although far apart of course, bravely, just as they had battled, each in his own way, up until now in this unhappy country. But Ivan Glavan would now no longer keep it up. He would up and go into captivity. They would hang him over an enormous anthill where the ants would begin with the soft parts of his body. Of course he also thought of his home, but that was far away, while the emperor was close by and they could have understood each other with a single glance, with the same kind of glance they had once shared in a far-off place called Rovenska.

22

Ever since the nightingales died, the emperor could not get enthusiastic about anything in this country, eventually not even about eau de cologne. He had no confidence in his generals, nor in the big landowners, nor in the monarchists, nor in the lonely buildings in which he spent the nights. He had no trust in the moist air he breathed, nor the low vault of the sky above him. He didn't trust the yellow fever to leave him alone. He did not even trust the Mexican plants anymore. Among his soldiers, he had found one quack from Styria who made him tea from sage that he had brought with him. He cleared his throat with this, and he drank schnapps infused with chamomile that had also been brought from home. Eventually he began to take pleasure in large quantities of dissolved garlic. This caused great difficulties around him, particularly because he had to take great care not to endanger his imperial dignity in Mexico.

This was quite difficult. It wasn't just the mixture of eau de cologne, wine, and now garlic that his entourage, accustomed by now to everything, had a more and more difficult time accepting. It wasn't just the birdcages that had to be carried on campaigns until the last of the birds died. It was that they were now running almost all the time. When they had to run from the capital, it was called a retreat. But when Juárez's forces pushed them back, when the French forces failed, and when the majority of the Austrian divisions were wandering in some desert near the Rio Grande or on the coast around Vera Cruz instead of being here, it became impossible to dissimulate. They still called it a tactical retreat, but it was really a flight, a full-fledged flight, even if it was on a quick and lively—but still a fleeing—white horse. Forced overnights on the haciendas of grandees alternated with stays in dirty army camps accompanied by the monotonous nightlong cries of guards and the howls of some kind of hyenas or nocturnal birds amid this foreign, truly foreign, land over which he was supposed to be the good father and ruler.

Maximilian knew: the vast majority of his forces were destroyed or else taken prisoner, which likely amounted to the same thing. Those that remained were exhausted, sick, badly provisioned, and without any desire to continue fighting a senseless war in a foreign, hopelessly foreign, country. The time was approaching when there would be nowhere left to run. Soon all roads to Vera Cruz would be cut off.

He was approaching the Capuchin monastery of San Francisco de la Cruz Querétaro. The only road out of it led to the Capuchin graveyard in Vienna.

23

The fate that had overtaken his beloved emperor had not yet overtaken the Austrian soldier from the scout company and former breakwater builder in Rovenska, Ivan Glavan. The republican forces did not leave their prisoners to the tigers, hyenas, and ants, nor did they cut off their noses and ears, nor did they roast them. And no one was hung over an anthill. After they surrendered, they were disarmed and locked up in a church. They were given water and maize gruel.

Over the next few months, Ivan Glavan did what he could have done at home, although there he would not have been in mortal danger and he would have been well paid. He led the works on an enormous field called Campo Austriaco for the republicans. The prisoners cut down trees, sawed wood, and worked the land. No longer were there rattlesnakes, cacti, or tigers here. Only yellow fever and maggots. Maggots that attacked all the food, as well as the carrion that would be crawling with them in an instant. It was said that these maggots carried yellow fever.

Yellow fever robbed them of the brave Corporal Gönhy and seven other soldiers. They died slowly, with horrible groans, rambling words about their homelands, and shouts of various women's names from all over the empire. The dying dreamed and moaned and called on Johannas, Elizabeths, Boženas, Mashas, Hildas, and many others whom they would never see again and who would never see them either.

Glavan groaned as well. Niguas had gotten into the wounds and scrapes he had acquired during the long campaign. This was a kind of sand flea that loved to burrow into open or wounded parts of the human body. They had gotten into his hands and feet, and a Mexican had to show him how to get them out. He and this Mexican quack surgeon made holes in his flesh and bored out these horrible tiny fleas, these niguas that had dug into his body.

The guards saw that there was no help for the prisoner. If the niguas didn't turn him into a piece of Swiss cheese, yellow fever would get him.

They left him at the edge of a forest, just as he used to leave dead foes. Now he was alone, as it had frequently been said: they will leave you like carrion, which is always in sufficient supply. And the tigers, hyenas, and vultures, as had been said, would thank them for their food. Now he, Ivan Glavan, would be that food, carrion, imperial carrion, and the vultures would have no trouble finding him at the edge of the forest, on some forest hillside not at all like the beech forest slopes of his native Slovenia, lying there with that head that had evoked such great respect and fear and that was now looking for a pillow on the roots of an enormous tree whose crown would provide a final resting place for his exhausted eyes.

24

As Ivan Glavan was boring insects out of his living flesh, the emperor was beginning a long journey that would end in the town called Querétaro: a journey that was still a journey of fate but not of great deeds. Juárez's forces had split the Austrian army, which was scattered over the vast country. Large companies and small groups were cut off from one another. Officers and their soldiers survived as best they could. It was only toward the end of '66 and at the beginning of '67 that Maximilian, or to be more exact his generals Mejía and Miramón, was able to gather a strong concentration of forces. But then the republican commander Porfirio Díaz marched with fourteen thousand men and one hundred cannon, smashed the imperial forces, and approached the angelic town of Puebla de los Ángeles. There were to be no more major battles. Little remained of imperial glory. All that remained were endless attempts to convince the French to act decisively to continue what they had begun, long letters to his brother in Europe with requests for reinforcements, and attempts to persuade his squabbling commanders, who were always on the edge of mutiny, of the need for unity in these difficult times. During the long nights he listened to stories about his soldiers, scattered all over this broad country, about men who had come from various European villages and towns and who, once here, had been killed by some other peasants in mountains and in forests. They had been hunted like big game, and then, when they had fallen behind, wounded and exhausted, they had been roasted on fires or even worse: they had been left to the wild beasts on forest hillsides. Did fate really want all of this? Did it want these horrible summers when the air quivered and time stood still, and when he sat on these hot evenings with his officers directing a war that did not move either? Or the freezing winters on mountain plateaus when he wrapped himself up in warm clothes and looked at the stars high in the sky hoping to find in them a great about-face? Or when he fled, when he fled again from Juárez's pitiless pursuers and crossed wild streams that carried off everything in their path? With ever-greater defeats, ever-greater treason, ever-greater spiritual wounds, ever closer to Querétaro.

25

In Querétaro rumors of detachments coming to help spread through the besieged imperial forces every day. And indeed, several commanders tried, on their own initiative, to break the broad ring that encircled Maximilian's final Mexican capital. Word also spread among the soldiers about the Slovene slaughterer who had risen from the dead. He had been abandoned, sick and exhausted, at the edge of a forest. But, together with a countryman by the name of Juretz, he had miraculously found his way to a monastery. There he had been helped and taken in by a passing Austrian detachment. Ivan Glavan, the emperor's dark and unknown shadow, who had journeyed thousands of miles across the ocean and all of Mexico, called by the same fate that had called his emperor, was again on the move, going automatically like some whale that swims to a certain beach or an eel that journeys to the Sargasso Sea. He was approaching Querétaro, killing and destroying everything in his path to his emperor. His enormous head, which continued to sow respect and fear in the enemy and which had long ago stopped evoking laughter among his comrades, had been glimpsed in Tlacotalpan. There, on a horse and with an ordinary bayonet in his hands, he had set a troop of Juárez's Indians to flight.

They were seized with dread when they saw above them some kind of god whose thin neck was topped by an unbelievably enormous head with sunken eyes. And the French newspapers, just like Vienna's *Die Presse,* again had something to report. At the battle near Sualtepec he was seen again in a cypress forest, where with his own hands he hung two republican generals, one mestizo and one small proprietor, from a high branch. He did this, as he told an American columnist, only because the soldiers of those generals had, the day before, cooked some wounded Austrians slowly over a low fire like suckling pigs. Then he disappeared together with General Figuera on a long campaign through Isatlán, Santa Cruz, and Aqua Sante, through Cocotitlán to Teotitlán. He used his engineering skills to construct bridges, and with his peasant perseverance he was able to overcome hunger and physical exhaustion. In the course of a long retreat, during which not a day passed without a skirmish or a nighttime attack, they lost four hundred men.

Whatever remained of Maximilian's army bled away in senseless marches, retreats, and skirmishes. The big battle they all expected, the one that would put an end to this constant retreating and dying, never took place. Near Acatlán yellow fever carried off Frank Juretz. Together with a comrade, Glavan buried him that same evening beneath a cactus and marked his grave with a heavy cross fashioned out of two hardwood logs, four feet high. In Acatlán they joined up with the units of Major Bernhart, who was accompanied by five companies of scouts and the Mexican colonel Troheker with two hundred lancers. Thus, after an immeasurably long period of time, Glavan again found himself in the Sierra Madre range. The enemy was approaching, this time with a gigantic army of thirteen thousand men, and it seemed that the decisive battle was finally at hand. That night, Glavan filled himself with an enormous quantity of pulque, and he told his comrades about his peasant people's age-old devotion to the imperial house, a devotion that had been proved in many battles on fields in Italy and Germany. He also bucked them up with tales about the slaughtering practices and the butcher business in his Slovene village. In the terrible battle that took place the next morning, the courageous Austrian soldiers charged up steep cliffs. For many minutes one could not hear the sound of a shot; only the rattle of bayonets and the cries and moans of the wounded rent the air. Here again Glavan's enormous head was seen, and it howled wolfishly in powerless rage when Major Bernhart and his uhlans and Colonel Troheker and his lancers fled like cowards. Before he found himself eye to eye with his beloved emperor in Querétaro with the cry of his fate and the fate of many dead men whom he had left in the Mexican plateaus with his own hands, before he found himself in Querétaro where their paths crossed again, he was seen in Puebla, defending that angelic city. His head, like an imperial banner on a thin neck, floated above the roofs and walls of that penultimate bastion of imperial forces.

26

Now things began to happen quickly, especially by local standards.

On April 2 Porfirio Díaz laid siege to the city of angels. By this point the emperor and a small detachment were completely cut off from the port of Vera Cruz. They had hesitated in escaping for so long that there was no longer any place to go. They locked themselves into Querétaro, and there, in its streets and in the cells and courtyard of its Capuchin monastery, they would play out the final scenes of the last great romantic and tragic story of the modern age. But, as it was a result of haughtiness and thoughtlessness, it is also a bit funny. And because of the incessant appeals to God's Providence and to fate, it is, in a way, an educational story with an accent on the irony of Providence.

Witnesses insist that Maximilian's fatal hour occurred well before the fall of Puebla. Marshal Bazaine, the commander of the French expeditionary force, offered to take him back to Europe. Supposedly, he began to think that he should take the advice and give up, but at the last minute he had a change of heart. Apparently he looked out across a plateau, because there was no ocean surface at hand, and again he discerned the call of fate appealing to him to do some great deed or other. Charlotte had gone to Europe instead of him, and she had begun to tell the European leaders that they should send help to Mexico. But eventually she had become lost in the labyrinth of the Vatican and of her own mind. In any case, nothing more could be done in Europe or in Mexico.

The siege of Querétaro began. Surviving eyewitnesses insist that the emperor could still have escaped.

But he could not bring himself to do it, say some. Others say he was prevented from doing so in some particularly mysterious way.

Escobedo, Juárez's plenipotentiary, offered him a way out. If he would abdicate the throne, the republican government would give him his life and allow him to escape along with General Mejía and his secretary, Blasio. According to partisans of one interpretation, Charlotte played a crucial role here. A letter of hers has been preserved, a letter Maximilian read frequently, supposedly on the night before the fall of Querétaro as well. She wrote: "Anyone who gives up writes his own certificate of incompetence. This can be forgiven only in old men and blockheads; but it is certainly impossible for a thirty-four-year-old prince, full of life and the future. At this moment, when you are taking the fate of the people into your hands, you have taken on risk and danger; you cannot abdicate this responsibility."

Maximilian loved these kinds of words. He had built his life around them: the fate of the people, taking on risk and danger.

He decided to stay.

27

As was the case with the life of the unhappy Charlotte, Maximilian's end also became fodder for many writers of literary works. The German author Karl May, who is well regarded for his authenticity and who made a careful study of the circumstances surrounding Maximilian's decision not to flee from besieged Querétaro, offers a different hypothesis: a Dr. Hilario was ordered to destroy the emperor's spirit, to prevent him from leaving Mexico, and to drive the empress insane through some mysterious potion. For various internal reasons Juárez had to have the emperor executed, but as a result he lost control and the government of Mexico fell into the hands of some secret lodges about which the writer is more or less silent. The conspiracy theory that May develops through endless plot twists is not the only one. Many commentators want to deprive Maximilian of his last remaining things—his belief in Charlotte's fateful letter, his hopes and dreams about God's Providence, which wanted things to develop and work out just as they did.

But even Karl May admits that there was something more powerful than the conspiracy of Hilario and his mysterious employers. For the last time, the emperor is told to run away before the enemy besieges Cerro de las Campanas. It seems he has finally made up his mind, and he steps toward the exit. Karl May writes, "But all of a sudden the emperor stopped: 'Forget about it,' he said with amazing tranquillity. 'The fate that lies upon me is more powerful. Now it is too late.' "

28

It is May 14. The emperor arrives in Cerro de las Campanas, which has practically been destroyed in the course of the siege. It can hold out for no more than a few hours. On May 15 the final division defending the emperor digs in at the monastery. The commander of the fort is Miguel López. The emperor believes in him. But it is actually Colonel López who betrays him and lets the republican army in through the monastery's stable doors. Many years later a scholar would say, "Miguel López did not betray him because of enmity toward his foreign imperial commander. He did not betray him out of love for the republican foe. He betrayed him because he was a traitor at heart. Even Mexicans consider him a traitor."

At seven o'clock the emperor sends out an emissary with an offer to surrender, and at eight he hands his sword to General Escobedo.

On May 21 the emperor has his final conversation with Escobedo. Now he is ready to accept what he had earlier refused. Once more, one final time, he has changed his mind. He says that he will abdicate the throne if in return they grant him his life and safe passage from the country for himself, his Austrian officers and soldiers, as well as for General Mejía and for his Mexican personal secretary, Blasio.

Escobedo refuses. The emperor continues to think for some time. His broad, deep eyes that had once looked into the distance are half closed. Through these narrow crevices he looks down at the floor, at the soil. The world has shrunk to this patch of mud on the well-trodden ground. Then he hands over his sword. Outside his soldiers are being disarmed, and some are being killed: it is the end.

29

On June 14, Emperor Maximilian and his generals Miramón and Mejía were sentenced to death by firing squad. The European powers protested, and the news arrived in Mexico from Rome that the Belgian princess Charlotte had completely lost her mind—she would remain insane for the rest of her days.

The monastery prison of Emperor Maximilian is a storeroom for garlic and onions. He awaits his final hour here amid a pile of rotting onions and garlic that emits a foul stench. He keeps thinking that this is all some terrible misunderstanding that will be fixed at any moment, but then the stink of decay again forces him to recognize that what is happening here looks like the end—only like decay and only like the end.

Juárez did not give in to threats or to requests to pardon the emperor. He was the son of an Indian peasant and a convinced republican. And he could never understand what this man had been doing in Mexico, or why so many people, including Austrians, had had to die because of this man. Despite all his blue blood, Ferdinand Max was for Juárez nothing but a trespasser. Not an emperor, merely an intruder. He had ordered republicans to be shot for to him they were rebels, outside the law. He had shot Mexicans like criminals, like dogs, the trespasser. And, in the end, Juárez was sick of his announcements that he would leave to be followed later by a change of mind because that is what, "ach, ja," fate had decided. Now there would be no more caprices, no more chances to change his mind.

"He can go," Juárez supposedly said, "but only in his coffin."

30

On June 19, Emperor Maximilian was taken from prison. Together with some guards he got into a cart. Mejía and Miramón got into a second cart.

All eyewitnesses agree that the emperor was driven off to death with his eyes staring toward the east. And when the cart turned from the main square toward the place of execution, the emperor turned his gaze toward the rising sun. Some say he was looking in the direction of his fatherland; others are convinced that in his thoughts he was across the sea, in Miramare, where the empress was wandering in her confused state amid the rooms and the gardens, blind to the beauty of her royal surroundings, as someone wrote. Looking toward that place he had left behind, toward the places where he had gotten bored laying cornerstones for ports and theaters, and from which he had departed for the sake of blind visions that he took to be the call of fate.

When, for a moment, he took his eyes from the ever more brilliant rays of the morning sunlight, Emperor Maximilian shuddered. Amid the crowd of people with coarse faces who were standing silently along his path with their caps in their hands or with their hands held in prayer, he noticed a man whose big head made him difficult to miss.

He saw an enormous head floating above all the others, and eyes that hid deep wellsprings in their sunken sockets. *Who is that,* he thought, *and where have I seen him?* The emperor glanced inquiringly at Glavan's enormous head, into the eyes of the dark shadow who had followed him, into the eyes of the butcher who had slaughtered for him in the Mexican plateaus and forests and who had been ready to die for him, to be burned by fire, or to dig niguas out of his skin. He who never betrayed anyone, because he was not a traitor, who was ever faithful, ever since a single moment on some distant island in a place whose name the emperor had long ago forgotten. Although he had been rather calm, Maximilian now shivered: that man had sideburns just like his, that creature, that *Wasserkopf* by the side of the road had hair on his enormous head that was parted like his, except that he was as big . . . as his older brother. So big . . .

His heart jumped. It was not his brother, nor was it some hallucination. This unnatural specter was he himself, Ferdinand Max. That was his other, enlarged, incredibly enlarged, macrocephalous, supernatural "I." *What is all this?* he thought. *What does it all add up to? Where have I forgotten some words?*

He tore his gaze from the sea and turned to the crowd, which had been following his speech carefully, to continue from the point when the flying fish had interrupted him, precisely when he had reached the part about greatness. Just then, instead of the adjutant who should have been nearby, and instead of the local bishop who was also supposed to be close at hand, he saw before him a completely impossible, somehow unnatural specter. For a moment he forgot where he was, here or somewhere else. Was he dreaming or was he really on a podium in some place whose name he had momentarily forgotten? In front of him stood a man with an enormous head, a truly powerful head that swayed on a thin neck in a tightly but-

toned collar. The man's hollow, sunken eyes gazed at him with doglike devotion and he was holding something out in front of him.

And Glavan also felt that a part of him was departing, irrevocably departing, a previously indivisible part of himself. And again he saw incorrectly when he caught that glance, missing the astonishment, the horror, the nausea, that had crept into that face amid the collapse and the rotting onions and garlic, the nausea caused by his subject's head with its dull and oafish eyes. He even forgave him for mispronouncing his name that time on Lošinj. He had said, "Just keep it up, Glavankopf." But Glavan saw only the gentle glance of his ruler, which was just the same as it had been when they laid the cornerstone together for the enormous construction project on some far-off island in the Adriatic Sea. He saw that, and his enormous, infinite subject's love and fidelity could not understand how it was possible that he was being led off to execution, and his enormous thankfulness for—he himself did not know for what; there was something incomprehensible here. And streams of water began to flow from Glavan's doglike devoted eyes, from the sunken eye sockets and their wellsprings. Down his stringy neck and into his high-buttoned shirt they flowed, from eyes that the emperor's glance had once triggered something in, lit on fire, calling them to the same fate.

He was holding something then, thought Emperor Maximilian. *He had something in his hand, some tool.* "Of course," he said, "the cornerstone, the cornerstone." *Just before that,* he thought, *just before that I saw the dolphins that leaped out of the water toward the sunlight. Those dolphins,* he thought, *it was in—what was the name of that place?*

31

Two days after Emperor Maximilian's death, the capital, Vera Cruz, surrendered unconditionally to Porfirio Díaz, and a few weeks after that the ship *Novara* under the command of Admiral Tegetthoff arrived to take the emperor's body and the remaining soldiers away. President Juárez had extended amnesty to all the Austrian soldiers and had sent them as directly as possible to Vera Cruz, from where they were to be transported to their far-off homeland. Some of them were also sent to Querétaro to witness the impartial trials meant to put an end to the senseless slaughter.

Of the approximately ten thousand Austrian Mexicanos, only 1,151 returned to their homes by April of the following year. Among them was one soldier whose enormous head evoked attention and induced mocking remarks. But the people pitied the majority of the poor wretches, who had left everything at home and even more, their health and all their hope, in Mexico. "How wretched they are, wrote the Ljubljana newspaper *Novice,* and it ended its article with the words: "The terrible outcome of the Mexican empire is this: the emperor has been executed and the empress is mad."

32

Maximilian's body was brought aboard ship on November 12. Six weeks later the ship sailed by the island of Lošinj. An unmistakable, big-headed man stood on the deck and looked in vain for the creeping tongue of the stone breakwater in Rovenska. The boat passed by the seaward side of the green island.

In the background was the snowcapped mountainous scenery; the sea shimmered by the shore. And on the other side of the island the mellow winter sun was shining on the breakwater and the cemetery, on that whole powerful absurdity.

He saw, floating above everything, the plume of the archduke Ferdinand Max, of the emperor Maximilian moving with dignity above all the people, above the crowns of the pines and above the bell tower. He saw it fluttering like an enormous bird that would fly up and circle above the island, the sea, and fly off toward the snow-covered mountains.

33

Ivan Glavan would spend the rest of his days among the quarry workers on the coast who were extracting blocks of marble for palaces in Milan, Vienna, and Cairo. From a thin spit of stone and sea he would watch boats sailing for all the corners of the world. Sometimes, he would look through the fence of Miramare Castle and see people promenading in the park, past the fountain he had built.

There he would also discover that the breakwater at Rovenska had, with great effort, actually been completed during the Mexican war.

But the port and the ship works had not been built, nor had bollards been attached to the breakwater. So no boats tied up there.

It was ascertained that an enormous and irreparable mistake had been made in the plans, and this had ruined some of the Lošinj captains and merchants.

The encyclopedia tells us tersely that the breakwater was built at the urging of a Captain Baričević, that it is two hundred meters long, and that it is raked by such powerful north winds that no one ever used it. The northeast winds are so strong here that waves break over the top. It is unclear how such experienced ship captains could have overlooked this crucial fact when they planned to build a port in Rovenska.

In the sea there remains a monument, a fallen stone obelisk that is here only to memorialize the pitiful and senseless fate of the man who laid the cornerstone. And those whose lives were caught up in that fate and who lie buried in the pine forest not far away, and those whose bodies have disintegrated in the damp of distant Mexican winters.

34

The tourists who sun themselves on it every summer sometimes think, if they think about anything at all, that the island is pleasantly green, that the sea is blue, and that if they are lucky they can see schools of dolphins swimming over the water's shiny surface. Sometimes it happens that a pair of lovers walks there in the spring, and then the woman, who has often had this thought, says, "What an amazing pier."

"It's not a pier," he says. "It's a breakwater."

"Still it's amazing," she says. "It has no bollards."

■ □ ■ □ ■

JOYCE'S PUPIL

Another of Joyce's pupils
was a young man of twenty named Boris Furlan.

Richard Ellman, James Joyce

I

This story will end with a mob dragging an old man with a weak heart—a retired professor and former law school dean—out of his house and loading him on a wheelbarrow as they cry out in anger and derision. He will be pushed through the winding streets of the old town toward the river, to be dumped into its rushing, freezing current.

The final lines of the story will be cried out in Slovene, in its upland, alpine dialect; mocking cries will resound on the street along which the wheelbarrow, with the bouncing helpless body on it, will rattle. A rain of imprecations, a beating shower of curses, a torrential flood of laughter, and a hail of furious abuse will fall upon the professor's head, the inside of which will suddenly go completely blank, as if swallowed by a black hole.

The chapter epigraph is from Richard Ellman, *James Joyce* (New York: Oxford University Press, 1982), 341.

2

The first lines are spoken many years earlier, in English, in the quiet of a Trieste apartment. It is evening. On the table one can see a warm circle of light, which radiates from a beautifully fashioned oil lamp. The thirty-year-old English teacher and his twenty-year-old pupil are bent over books and papers. A strong north wind is blowing outside, searching for a route through the streets to the sea. Shutters bang and the sea foams against the shore; the swirling winds only accentuate the tranquillity and safety of the room. The pupil reads English sentences aloud, and the teacher patiently corrects his pronunciation. When the lesson is over, the teacher walks to the window and looks out onto the street, where a piece of paper blows and eddies in the wind. Perhaps he speaks in his Irish accent about the language, perhaps about Thomas Aquinas. After each lesson pupil and teacher generally discuss philosophy. The pupil, like so many youths of the day, is much taken with Schopenhauer and Nietzsche. The teacher attempts to quell this enthusiasm; for him, the only philosopher is Aquinas, whose thought, in the teacher's opinion, is as sharp as a sword blade. The teacher reads a page of his work in Latin every day.

Then the teacher sits back down and asks the pupil to describe the oil lamp in English. The pupil gets hopelessly tangled in technical expressions, and the teacher takes over from him, describing the oil lamp in exhaustive detail. He goes on for a full half hour, indulging a habit that many years later the student will call descriptive passion.

"Professor Zois," the student cries out, "I will never learn English."

Professor Zois chuckles, in part out of satisfaction at his description, in part at the way the pupil mangles his name. That is how the Italians say it because they can't pronounce *Joyce* properly.

3

After this conversation by the light of the oil lamp, Joyce's pupil, a young Slovene law student from Trieste, suddenly felt a certain blankness in his head. A moment before he had been speaking freely with his teacher about Schopenhauer and Aquinas, about problems of morality and courage, but when he was confronted with the puzzle of the oil lamp, the fuel well, the glass chimney, the wick, and all the rest of the parts that made up that insignificant object, he felt a gigantic hole opening up inside his head, a hole that swallowed up every thought, a kind of empty space in which nothing could be heard but the howl of the wind through the Triestine streets on the way to the sea. The wind was growing stronger and beginning to roar to the sound of the voluptuously ornamented, albeit somewhat monotonous, speech of Professor Zois, which emanated from the depths of his descriptive passion. And the gathering storm was also accompanied by the roars, howls, and clamor of a gigantic crowd.

4

Joyce and his Triestine student met for the last time on a hot July day in the summer of 1914. One could feel tension in the air throughout the city. Mobilized men were mustering near the barracks, while crowds shouting bellicose slogans milled on the streets and piazzas. The teacher, upset and worried, rapped on his young friend's apartment door. Then they looked through the windows of the pupil's room at the building of the Italian consulate, which was surrounded by an angry crowd. Encouraged by loud shouts, several of them tried to tear down the Italian flag. Stones were thrown at the facade, some panes of glass shattered, there was yelling. Joyce was clearly perturbed, and he worriedly asked his young friend what was going to happen.

"Professor Zois," he said with a laugh, "there will be war."

This scared his teacher. Joyce said that he would depart. When the shouts of the crowd grew louder he shut his eyes, then he turned around, and while his pupil was still speaking he ran out of the apartment and the building without saying a word. The pupil laughed; history was being made outside. He understood that some people can derive ineffable joy from describing an oil lamp, but he was interested in other things. The roar of the crowd heralded the arrival of momentous times. He was drawn outside, into the whirlwind.

5

In the years that followed, the pupil developed into a determined and contented man. He succeeded at everything he started. His mind, which had been unable to comprehend his teacher's passion for description, inclined to analytic passions; Kant, Croce, and Masaryk were stacked on his desk. He received his law degree from the University of Bologna. And he was attracted ever more strongly to the nervous agitation of European events, which whirled across the piazzas of Trieste like an Adriatic storm. Four years after his teacher, frightened by the tumult of the crowd, had run from his apartment (and, soon after, from Trieste and his pupil's life), he was eyewitness to a new historical twist. On a gray November afternoon Italian troops disembarked in the port of Trieste. And not too long after this a new set of specters appeared on the streets. Young men from Italian suburbs and small towns marched about in black uniforms singing of youth and springtime; they beat their political opponents and set fire to a large building in the center of town—the Slovenian National Hall. When firemen came to fight the blaze, they cut their hoses to the sounds of bellicose slogans. The young lawyer tried to settle down in the midst of the blind tumult of history. He opened a law practice, continued to read in philosophy and science, but he could not evade the angry times so characteristic of beaten Europe, the passionate crowds that gathered beneath the balconies, or the pursuit of the secret police. He found himself among those educated Slovenes of Trieste who organized anti-Fascist resistance. In 1930 he was warned that his arrest was imminent. He escaped over the border into Yugoslavia and in a single day found himself in a new city among new people. In the thick fog that curled through the streets of Ljubljana that fall, his inner vision searched for the far-off and now-lost shining disk of Trieste's sun, and his inner ear listened to the howling of an Adriatic storm. With a beating heart he read newspaper accounts of the convictions of his fellow Slovenes, whom the Fascist courts sent to distant Sicilian prisons or to local villages under armed guard. There was something about this agitated time, this agitated atmosphere, that his analytic mind could not understand. He told his friends that when reading accounts of these political trials, he sometimes felt a kind of emptiness in his head, something like what used to happen when he had to describe the details of a lamp for his teacher Joyce.

6

It was to the light of a completely different lamp, a modern and electric one in the quiet reading room of the university library, that, in the middle of January 1941, he was leafing through the English newspapers, which regularly carried accounts of the latest trials in Trieste. His glance was suddenly halted and numbed by a story from which he learned that James Joyce had died in Zurich. He was surprised to discover from this article that his former English teacher, the interesting and to his lawyerly mind somewhat eccentric Professor Zois, had become a rather well-known writer in the intervening years. He resolved to read his books and wondered where he would get hold of them, since the author was practically unknown here. He did not know that he would soon find them where they were quite popular—in England.

But now was not a time for reading; events followed one after another, history thickened. There was great agitation among immigrants from Trieste, for all of them knew what awaited them if Slovenia was taken by Italian troops.

As in November 1918, in the spring of 1941 he again observed the arrival of their forces. This time the army did not disembark. Now they rolled in, and through the dusty streets of Ljubljana came motorized divisions, infantry, and horses dragging artillery pieces, the barrels of which never fired a shot during the campaign of conquest. For the army of the country they rolled through had disintegrated all by itself.

By the time officers of the Italian secret police knocked at his apartment door, he was in Switzerland, taking a tram along the narrow and peaceful Zurich street up the hill to the cemetery. While his Ljubljana apartment was being turned upside down, he was standing at the grave of his former English teacher.

"Professor Zois," he said, and he could hear his laugh, and see him as he stepped to the window and looked out at the sea. There was no sea here, but far below was Lake Zurich, and it seemed to him that he could also hear that howling of the storm outside his window, winds that carried up to him the roar of the crowds in the harbor. But down below no troops were disembarking; tourists were getting off boats onto the wooden pier.

When, several days later, he got onto the train in Zurich that was to take him to Paris, an Italian court was convening in Ljubljana. In a session that took less time than did his trip to the French border, he was sentenced to death in absentia.

7

In May of that same year he was dropped off at his hotel by a Serb, a representative of the Yugoslav government in exile in London. Sirens were wailing on that warm and peaceful evening. His driver jumped into the car and drove off quickly together with his suitcase. People were running on the street, and a man with a band on his sleeve pushed him into a bomb shelter. In the basement he heard the echoes of explosions, and through the basement window he saw a piece of glowing sky. Incendiary bombs were falling on the city beneath the vault of an evening May sky. Somewhere close by, the piece of glowing sky that he saw was marked by the bright lines of antiaircraft fire. Then it turned out that the man who was standing next to him and calmly smoking a cigarette was the receptionist at the hotel where he was supposed to stay. The receptionist said that once again there would be no electricity, and that they would again be using kerosene or oil lamps. In that London basement, in the midst of an air raid, Joyce's pupil rocked with irrepressible laughter. He asked the receptionist to tell him how a lamp like that worked. The man was not surprised at the question, for his job was such that he had heard everything. So he lit another cigarette and began to explain. And thus he spent his first London evening, until the attack had ended, with that receptionist yielding to the descriptive passion, hearing about the workings of oil lamps, which turned out to be a bit different in London from Trieste.

He fell asleep in his small hotel room toward morning, fully clothed on his bed. While he slept, he dreamed that he was diving into the ocean near Trieste.

8

His voice became famous in Slovenia. It was the voice of Radio London. His words were clear and determined, a call for resistance. He spoke of the German defeats in Africa and in Russia. He announced the landing in Sicily, narrated the battle for Monte Cassino, and with triumphant satisfaction proclaimed the capitulation of Italy. His voice, emanating from radio speakers, was listened to after curfew behind shuttered windows in city apartments, while the muffled steps of German night watchmen echoed through the streets. The partisans in liberated territories listened to him; their adversaries could hear him as well. His speech "Plain Speaking from London" was printed as a pamphlet and dropped from Allied planes over Slovenia in 1944. Here he called on the Slovenian Home Guard to join the Partisan resistance. In the Slovene press, which appeared with the approval of the occupation authorities, he was called the Bawler from London.

By now he had been completely swallowed up by the whirlwind of history. One evening when, exhausted, he was shuffling papers in the London studio by the light of a desk lamp, he told a colleague that he would return. He would join the Partisans. His colleague warned him that everything there had been taken over by the Communists, but the Bawler from London rebutted him sharply. On that very evening the colleague wrote in his wartime diary: "He is an honorable and sincere person, I think, but hopelessly naive."

By February 1945 he was on territory liberated by the Partisans, and a few months later he was back in Ljubljana. When new people took power he was named dean of the law school. Two years later he was arrested.

9

"With a little bit of imagination," the interrogator said, "one could say that it was that James guy (or whatever you call him) who got you into this whole mess." Joyce's pupil was sitting at a table, a glowing shaft of pale light poured into his wide-open eyes. On the table was a lamp; its powerful electric light illuminated his whole face. The red end of a lit cigarette circled behind him, and it moved in rhythm with the laughing lips, which emanated puffs of white smoke.

"He taught you English," the investigator laughed, "and had you not known English, you would not have become a British spy."

"I am not a spy," said Joyce's pupil.

"You are a spy," said the voice out of a cloud of smoke. He told him this every evening and every night. And they spent many nights in that dark room, in the blinding circle of light through which the white traces of cigarette smoke could be seen.

"You frequented the English consulate," he said. The light was white and sharp, and circles burned in his eyes. Joyce's pupil recalled the oil lamp, and its circle of warm, yellowish light.

"We're finished," said the interrogator. "Now you can go back to your cell. Tomorrow you'll go to be shaved, and then to trial."

"I am not a spy," said Joyce's pupil.

"You are a spy," came the voice from behind the circle of light. "You are a traitor. And you will be sentenced to death."

Joyce's pupil went pale. It seemed to him that he could hear the roar of the sea whipped up by an Adriatic storm.

"I was sentenced to death once before," he said quietly.

"That was in absentia," laughed the interrogator. "This time you will be present."

10

That was on a hot July evening in 1947. They led him through a labyrinth of corridors and doors, each of which closed behind him. Back to his cell, as narrow as a closet—six paces long, two wide. All night long a light burned high on the ceiling; its red light danced in his eyes through his rough blanket, preventing him from sleeping. Behind that brightness, in his inner vision that was hidden from the light, deep in his head, deep down where time and space could be conquered, he saw a series of agitated images of Trieste piers, foggy Ljubljana streets, and even foggier London streets.

Toward morning, toward the bright July morning that somehow managed to penetrate through his somnambulant state, he heard footsteps and loud voices from the street outside. The city streets were just beyond the walls of the Ljubljana prison, and people were heading to work. He got up just as he heard keys rattling. The barber was at the cell door. The boom of footsteps and voices multiplied outside, growing ever louder, a murmuring multitude of humanity. Around the court building a crowd of righteous people was gathering to express their solidarity with the prosecutors who, in the name of the people, were about to begin the trial of the traitors, turncoats, spies, and enemies.

From the waiting room he looked out onto a sea of heads, which was being moved back and forth by an invisible force, some kind of invisible and inaudible wind. For an instant he saw himself and his teacher, that was the last image before they led him into the hall: they were standing by the window of his Trieste apartment, he was twenty years old, and a crowd outside was yelling and hurling rocks at the Italian consulate. His teacher no longer had any kind of descriptive passion, and he was afraid—he wanted to run away, and he ran away. The pupil had laughed. Now it was July 1947 and he was not laughing. Now he was afraid—he too would have run away. But there was nowhere to go. There was only one way, and it led through a labyrinth of corridors and doors into the law court.

II

All of the accused looked like shadows. They were worn out, they hadn't slept, and they were anxious. The hall was filled with people who greeted them with an ominous murmur. They were seated on the front bench, and arrayed behind them and along the walls were uniformed guards. The stenographers waited with their hands on their knees. Sharpened pencils lay on the desks, motionless as loaded guns.

The trial lasted for two weeks, from morning until night with a break for lunch. The sharp speeches of the prosecutors and the stammering of the accused were broadcast out onto the square in front of the courthouse and into other squares and streets throughout Ljubljana. All over the country working people gathered around radio speakers and listened to the thunder of the prosecutor's speeches: Some part of the Slovene intelligentsia has always been in foreign service. They have always sold themselves and been hopelessly fascinated by things foreign, especially foreign money. Full-page articles in the newspapers described the trial: Nothing has brought so much unhappiness, blood, martyrdom and suffering to the people as this small reactionary clique. Naked treason in the pay of foreigners is in the dock. They are being tried not merely by working people but by all men, by all humanity, wrote the *Slovenian Courier.*

On the sixth or seventh day the prosecutor deposed Joyce's pupil. He spoke of the book *Animal Farm* that the accused had received from England. According to the prosecutor, he had made vile use of his knowledge of English, acquired in Trieste, to translate excerpts from this loathsome pamphlet, and he had lent the book to his fellow conspirators. A hush fell when he asked the accused to describe the contents of this book. The hush radiated out through the microphones to the crowd in front of the law court. His silence gaped through the radio speakers, and the next day a newspaper described it as the poor and tortured silence of an impenitent man. At last the accused spoke.

"Describe it," he moaned. "I can't describe it. In my head," he said.

"In your head?" shouted the prosecutor.

After a long pause the accused added, "In my head there is a kind of emptiness."

"As he himself asserts, there is an emptiness in his head," the prosecutor said calmly and triumphantly. And the people in the hall stirred, laughter coursed through the square in front of the court, and the entire crowd began to applaud the prosecutor's words, as the daily news reported in big headlines the next day.

Beneath a lamppost to which a microphone was attached, an old man leaned over to his wife. "If he hadn't been moaning so, I'd say that his voice was familiar," he said. "Isn't that the Bawler from London?"

12

On August 12 the chief justice announced the verdict. The three accused were sentenced to death by firing squad, with confiscation of all their property and permanent loss of political and civil rights. The hall applauded. The face of one of the judges showed that he was sickened by the applause. He lifted his hand to quiet the people, but when the hall calmed down, one could hear applause like an echo from the outside and then loud approval from the gigantic square, which had been occupied from early morning by a crowd of people that had gathered to hear the announcement of the verdict.

13

When they brought him to his cell, a piece of paper awaited him. They told him that he could write home or to whomever he wished.

He lay down on his bed and looked up at the ceiling. That evening they turned out the light, for the first time in many months. Guards looked into his cell at intervals.

14

He lived for the next two years in solitary confinement, although he was allowed to read there. Sometimes, late at night, his former interrogator came to sit by his bunk. One night he asked whether he thought that from a strictly juridical point of view his punishment had been just. He did not answer; he just turned to the wall. Another time his nocturnal visitor wanted to know what had happened during the trial. Why had he not described the contents of the book? Where had the sudden emptiness in his head come from?

"It is all because I do not possess the descriptive passion," said the former law school dean. The interrogator gave him a strange look, worriedly shaking his head.

Toward the end of the next year he was told that he had been given amnesty. Instead of the death penalty he had been sentenced to twenty years in prison. Four years later he was paroled because of heart trouble. He settled down in a small upland city. All night a light burned in his window. In the mornings he looked up at the shining white alpine peaks. He spoke rarely, and his movements were slow and unnatural.

15

One evening in late autumn 1953 he heard footsteps and commotion in front of his house. He turned off the desk lamp, walked to the window, lifted up the curtain, and at that instant he felt an icy shudder course through his entire body. A dark clump of people was outside, and they were preparing to do something. Someone called out his name. Someone shouted, "He wants to sell Trieste to the Italians! Him and his English friends." Blows rang out against the door, grumbling male voices were in the foyer, and a moment later they were in his room, which was immediately filled with bodies, with the smell of sweat and alcoholic fumes.

Powerful hands grabbed him and pulled him out of the house and onto the street. They loaded him on a wheelbarrow. The wheelbarrow bounced on the pavement on its way down to the river.

The procession was accompanied by bursts of laughter and shouts: "Speek Eengleesh, speek Eengleesh!" The iron wheel of the wheelbarrow bounced on the pavement, the helpless body flew up like a sack, and the professor felt that his weak heart was going to stop. With shaking hands he tried to shield his eyes from the faces that leaned over him, from the mocking and the senseless hail of curses: "You old fool, old fool." "Judas, traitor." Whenever the wheelbarrow stopped to allow the man pushing it to spit into his palms before beginning again, lips spewing alcoholic vapors bent down to him: "Where are your English friends now?" And the question was answered by the yodeling laughter of women and the grumbling guffaws of men: "Speek Eengleesh, speek Eengleesh."

16

Before the iron wheel of the wheelbarrow set off down the street again, before the ecstatic procession could start up, the old man lifted his arms and fluttered his hands, trying to tell them something. As if he himself had finally understood something. The shaking after this fluttering produced even more humorous smirks.

And even before they reached the riverbank, their cheers, snarls, and guffawing laughter had turned into a distant roar. That roar resounded in the same emptiness that took over his head like a black hole, like the impossibility of further description. Now it seemed to the professor that with his juridical brain and his analytic passion he had finally come to understand the meaning of the emptiness that appeared in the face of the impossibility of description. That is why his helpless body no longer felt the rain of mockery that was falling on him, did not take in the hail of curses that beat on him, did not react to the flood of laughter that broke over him, and did not hear the stream of furious insults. That is to say, the monotonous and distant roar took place outside of his head and its emptiness, its hollow space. It was, in fact, no longer the meaningless roar of ever-new crowds that wailed and howled like an Adriatic storm through the streets of Trieste to the sea. It was an approaching roar. And in the distance, in some endless space, it grew out of a single word, a word neither

Slovene nor English that had never been written down in any language, a word that had never been spoken or used to describe anything, a word that could say everything, although neither teacher nor pupil could utter it, a word comprehensible in its incomprehensibility but one that neither teacher nor pupil would ever be able to use. This was what he would have wanted to tell his former teacher, for he had come to understand that there is a word at the beginning and the end, and that that word has nothing to do with the language in which it is spoken or written.

That is why he fluttered his hands, and why the uplanders laughed even more joyfully and shouted even more loudly: "Speek Eengleesh, speek Eengleesh."

He no longer heard them, only the distant roar, and he didn't know by now whether it was the booming of the sea, or of the crowd, or whether it was the storm itself outside his windows amid whose gusts could be heard Professor Zois's monotonous voice describing an oil lamp.

■ □ ■ □ ■

TWO PHOTOGRAPHS

Fate likes repetition, variation, symmetry . . .
He is killed, but he does not realize that he is dying so that a scene can be repeated.

Jorge Luis Borges

It is thought that people live in a kind of underground cave . . .
Whoever is intelligent knows that his eyes can fail twice and for two reasons: the first time when we step from light into darkness and the second when we go from darkness into light. Whoever then says that the same is true of the soul would never begin to laugh unreasonably if he saw that the soul was confused.

Plato, The Republic, *VII*

The Old Lady

On this side the square is practically empty. Roars, shouts, and the wailing of sirens come from far away, from beyond the monument, from the upper part of the enormous square. A few people stand around here in front of the stores and among the trees; they chat and they all look in the direction of the monument. An old woman dressed in black comes across the white pavement, moving slowly across the enormous empty space. She holds her arms close to her chest, as if wading through water, a clumsy handbag hangs over her elbow, and in her other hand she clutches some light-colored thing, as if afraid that the wind might carry off whatever she is carrying. She is clearly exhausted. She walks across the sidewalk as if climbing a flight of stairs. For a moment she looks down at the ground, then she lifts her glance and slowly turns to the nearest tree. For a moment it seems to the man standing somewhere in the shadows shifting his weight back and forth that the old lady is walking toward him. He glances at her out of the corner of an eye and then again turns his nervous glance toward the monument from which some figures run across the square. The old lady leans against the tree with both hands and again looks down at the ground. Her bag swings like a weight in the empty space. She lifts the hand that holds the light-colored paper up the tree trunk as if wanting to protect it from a flood or from the wet ground she sees beneath her. The man looks at the figures running across the square and listens to the shouting from the other side that becomes ever louder and more confused. Suddenly he raises his hand and waves. Then he says something out loud. Someone in the crowd stops and looks about. The man calls out again. Now another man looks around in confusion, sees him, and heads quickly toward the trees. In his hands he's holding a camera, and there's a big leather bag over his shoulder; it must be very heavy and it gets in the way as he walks.

Then the photographer stands next to the man and explains something to him in animated tones. They both look toward the monument and again the man sees the old lady out of the corner of his eye. She seems somehow smaller than before. The old lady is sliding down the tree trunk. She clings to the rough bark with both hands. She grasps the paper tightly in her fist with her fingers, and her knuckles chafe against the tree bark. The pavement is cold and wet. She lies down, for her legs are no longer strong enough. Then she sees the crowns of the trees high above, and some tall buildings behind them. It is as if she is lying at the bottom of a deep pit surrounded by trees and by the bright facades beyond them. The man looks at the crowd running across the square. There are ever more of them and the person next to him sets up his camera. And simultaneously he realizes that something is missing; the old lady has disappeared.

"The old lady," the man says, "that old lady has fallen down."

The Mothers of the Plaza de Mayo

The photographer who ran across the square and set up his camera next to the man on the pavement knows every type of demonstration like the back of his hand. He plies his trade in one of the most politicized countries on earth. Especially in recent years, since the fall of the latest putschist government, which like many predecessors ruled for only a short time, not a week has gone by without the Plaza de Mayo resounding with the footsteps of demonstrators. And that is why there are men who spend every day in front of the Casa Rosada with cameras that, thanks to modern communications technology, can send their messages to every corner of the world in an instant. Amid the monotonously repetitive leftist and rightist and joint meetings and demonstrations, amid the sum of their radical and moderate and mixed demands and messages, there had recently appeared unusual pictures of women, sometimes screaming and at moments even shrieking inarticulately while at others maintaining a dignified silence. Unexpectedly, those photographs had suddenly become extremely valuable on the international communications marketplace. The news media and the pundits who form public opinion quickly found a suitable name for this unusual group of demonstrators: the mothers of the Plaza de Mayo. It is hard to figure out why the photographs of these women became such a hot commodity in the international media jungle. It is not enough to note their connection with the dirty war in which some thirty thousand opponents of the military regime had disappeared. After all, those years marked only one episode, one chapter of a long war, merely one scene from a political bedlam that has been going on for almost three hundred years. Many of the disappeared had been found in deep pits, in mass graves that had begun to be uncovered all over the country, and for the most part it had been impossible to identify their remains. Some people claimed that ten thousand had been killed, while others were convinced that there were at least thirty thousand *desaparecidos*. But the public was already inured to the corpses, which of course were exhumed and displayed in photographs and on television screens as well. The public, which one imagines sitting in a comfortable armchair with a beer and some salty snacks, can by now see corpses from every corner of the world every evening, as it were. Those corpses wear various uniforms and clothing, and they are of various races, sizes, ages, and sexes. But the public woke up when they saw the mothers from the Plaza de Mayo, with their tearful and shrieking faces and with the photographs of their lost sons in their hands or pinned to their blouses. The mothers who were demanding the return of their sons still had some hope. Their sons were on the lists of the *desaparecidos,* though no one could tell them anything reliable about their fate, whether they were lying in some pit or whether by some miraculous chance they were still alive, locked either in jail or in some other hidden place. In terms of politics it was impossible to classify the movement of these sobbing women, their crying and waving hands. The women were simply not interested in anything except their sons. Their faces on the screen seemed aggrieved and desperate but nevertheless hopeful. Perhaps it was that fact, if not its terrifying background, that forced the public to stay in their chairs for a while before heading to the refrigerator for another beer. And perhaps that explains why for a short time photographs of that group of women from the Plaza de Mayo were so desirable.

The photographer rummaged nervously in his bag, hastily exchanged a few words with the man on the pavement, and focused his lens. Then he stepped forward a bit, leaned on the tree, and took some shots of some of those running toward the back of the pack, those who had joined the demonstrators and were being chased by the police. The man standing in the shadows called out to him.

"The old lady," he called out, "that old lady has fallen down."

Photographs of Two Desaparecidos

The man runs toward the old woman who is lying on the ground and tries to lift her. He can see that the woman is conscious, for she is looking at him with her nervous eyes and the hand, the hand that clutches the two photographs, is stretched out in front of her.

"She's in bad shape," he calls out to the man with the camera.

"Señora," he says, "señora, are you sick?"

He reaches under her arms and lifts the old lady up so that she is sitting on the pavement with her handbag in her hands. She is pale and he sees that she is about to faint.

"Bring some water," he calls out toward the trees, where the other man is now leaning up against the trunk, camera glued to his eye, pointing his lens toward the last rows of demonstrators. They are running toward the bishop's palace and looking for a clear escape route. The photographer looks around undecidedly, then continues to snap.

"A cup of water, Alberto," shouts the man who is now holding the woman like a sack in his arms. Her limp legs are extended along the pavement; she is completely powerless, embracing her handbag and clutching the photographs in her hand. Alberto waves his hand and then returns to his camera again. Now the square is full of figures. The police, arms extended, are trying to catch them as if playing a game of tag. A small dark-haired man has been pressed up against a paddy wagon and is being beaten with a nightstick. From the other end of the square the screams of women can still be heard; no one has touched them, but a jettylike iron wall of policemen is keeping them away from the government building. Some young men in the back are chosen and dragged into cars. The majority of the group crowds around the monument. By now the man has managed to move the woman, her bag hanging over her shoulder; he takes her under the arms and slowly leads her toward a bench. The old lady collapses. The square slowly empties. Alberto puts the camera away and places his heavy leather bag on the bench next to the woman. Then he runs off somewhere and returns with a glass of water.

The man puts the edge of the glass to her lips. The old woman drinks little gulps. The man moistens her forehead and temples.

"You ruined my shoot," Alberto says with a sigh.

"It's always the same," says the man.

"Today was a bit more lively," Alberto says.

"You would have left her lying on the ground," says the man.

"After everything I've seen, my dear fellow," says Alberto, standing up and looking around to see whether things have bubbled up again or whether something new has begun. But there is nothing. The square is even emptier and even the yelling has quieted down.

The sounds of the receding police sirens can be heard from the nearby streets.

"It doesn't matter," says the man. "You can't just let her lie on the ground." Alberto sits down again and only now does he look carefully at the old lady sitting between them.

"Ah," he says, "now I know who she is. She's here every day. I know you, señora."

The old lady looks at him and nods.

"She's lost two," he says. "Two disappeared."

He beckons toward her hands with his chin.

"Take a look, she has pictures."

"Can I have a look, señora?" the man asks politely while reaching for the photos. The woman slowly opens her fist. The man takes the two photos and sees the image of a blond young man sitting with crossed legs on a wicker sofa. He's wearing an open, light-colored shirt. He smiles, as if the person who took the photograph had just told him something funny.

"Your son?" he asks.

The old lady nods.

Then he looks at the image of another young man. He looks similar. He is wearing a military uniform.

"His brother?" he asks.

The old lady shakes her head.

"Not his brother," says Alberto.

"Your son?" the man asks.

The old lady shakes her head.

"Leave her be," says Alberto, "she doesn't know Spanish. She's out of her mind," he says. "She walks around the Plaza de Mayo and shows everyone the pictures. She speaks some Slavic language, Russian or something like that. Then an old priest comes along and leads her away. But the woman always comes back the next day."

"What kind of uniform is that, anyway?" the man asks.

Alberto takes the photograph and looks at it.

"I don't know," he says, "it could be German. The photograph's an old one. Maybe it's Polish."

"It's not Polish," says the man.

"Then it's German," says Alberto. "It doesn't matter."

The old lady looks at the picture that is being passed back and forth before her eyes, carefully watching it and following it with some hand gestures.

"OK, but what does this soldier have to do with the *desaparecidos*?"

"How would I know?" says Alberto. "The lady is a little mixed up. I'm telling you she's not exactly right in the head. Just look at how she's watching us."

Alberto stands up and again opens his heavy camera bag.

"The old man is coming," he says. "He'll lead her away. Let's get going."

"Good-bye, señora," says the man. "Now everything will be all right, won't it?" He chuckles pleasantly. The old lady nods. A gray-haired man walks toward them. He is wearing dark clothing with a priest's collar around his neck, in heavy boots with thick soles. They wave at him.

"Where are you parked?" Alberto asks.

"No, it's not German either, I know what German emblems look like."

"So what?" says Alberto. "Where are you parked?"

The priest sits down next to the lady, takes her by the hand, and says something to her. The old lady nods. Then she puts both photographs into the handbag that is now on her knees. They get up and slowly cross the Plaza de Mayo, where the evening paseo is beginning.

The First Photograph—The Young Man in a Light-Colored Shirt

Until the moment when a push of the button tripped the camera's shutter and captured his smile, preserving him in a snapshot sitting on a wicker sofa in a garden somewhere wearing a light-colored shirt with his legs crossed, until that moment we can say nothing that would help us to understand the arc of Gojmir Blagaj's life, the surprising and powerful events that were to follow, events that the old local priest, in all his rustic simplicity and gravity would call a devil's brew. And with that simple statement he would be thinking about even more than he could express. He would be thinking about a devilish plot that the Prince of Darkness had been organizing for a long time in some faraway country and then repeating here with other people. Up until that moment even he, a parish priest from a lowland village, could not have told us anything, though he certainly knew the young man, had worried over his spiritual development, had watched over him and spoken with him about his most intimate affairs. Nothing other than the fact that from the time he was seventeen the young man had frequently told him that he could not find meaning in anything he had begun, from his schoolwork to hiking in the mountains on the other side of the country. But as far as the old man was concerned, all young people were like that. Some of them want one thing, others another, perhaps even something higher, more exciting, bolder. And then they calm down. But in this he was mistaken. The young man sitting on the sofa next to him and smiling at some girl holding a camera in her hands would not calm down, because his restlessness went deeper than the old man could imagine. The young man is twenty-five, and behind him are many years of living with his mother, college, the army, and monotonous hours and days in the bank where he worked as a loan assessor. Ahead of him are people, events, and meetings that he would be unable to avoid.

In the photograph that the reporter on the Plaza de Mayo would look at with professional nonchalance a decade later, he is laughing, in an open light-colored shirt, sitting on a wicker sofa. The garden is sultry and hot, and above their heads is a thin and diaphanous humid haze that makes breathing difficult. The garden is close to a city that long ago someone named Nuestra Señora María de Buenos Aires.

Ada

A few months after that garden pastoral, Gojmir becomes acquainted with Ada. Given that when she pushed through the crowd of people at the entrance she could easily have turned to someone else, their meeting was unexpected and surprising, dizzying and completely accidental. Even later she couldn't say why precisely she had walked up to him.

The morning hours are drawing to a close. The woman who had been sitting across from Gojmir, turning around in her revolving chair, had gotten up and walked out across the large bank lobby with a pleasant smile on her face. The marble lobby is filled with people walking here and there, the majority crowding around the entrance. For the last two hours the calls and footsteps of students have been echoing from the nearby university building. In addition, a distant roaring sound could be heard that at times grew and then quieted down for a long time. The wailing of police sirens sliced through these sounds. The clients are waiting for the street to empty while the employees look nervously at the clock as siesta time approaches. Gojmir Blagaj is writing down some information and filling in the blank sections of the forms that the woman had left on his desk. When he lifts up his glance, he notices a young woman who had pushed through the crowd at the entrance, looked around the room, and a moment later walked toward him. Gojmir thinks that it is his customer who had forgotten something on his desk, but at that same moment he realizes that it is a different young woman coming toward him. A young lady wearing jeans and carrying a bundle of books that she holds with arms crossed against her chest. She sits down calmly on the empty revolving chair as if she had been there for some time.

"I'd like some information," she says. She sits stock-still, but Gojmir notices that she can't control her gaze. She turns her head slightly to one side and looks at the door out of the corner of her eye. She starts visibly when a man in a light, bright-colored jacket with sweat stains under his armpits and a loose tie comes rushing through the crowd by the door.

"If I am not mistaken," Gojmir says with a smile, "someone is looking for you."

The girl looks at him in amazement and tries to chuckle. Her lips tremble a bit at the edge of her mouth. Gojmir leans toward her and pushes a piece of paper into her hand. The man walks around the lobby and looks at the teller lines. Gojmir smiles and begins to talk about interest rates. He is amazed at his calm smile, and it seems to him that he is seeing his own smiling face in a mirror. He is amazed at the calm image, though he can feel precisely the wild beating of his heart. His colleague at the next table looks at them carefully. The man in the bright jacket runs into someone and apologizes politely. The sounds on the street disperse into separate cries, and the people by the door go through it.

"Don't look around now," says Gojmir, "your acquaintance is leaving." The woman looks steadily at a spot on the paper and does not move for a little while.

"OK," said Gojmir, "he's gone."

"Thanks," says the woman, and her facial expression softens.

"I'd like to sit here for a bit," she says. "My name is Ada. In fact Adelina and my brother's name is Anselmo. It's funny, isn't it?" she says.

"Why should it be funny?" asks Gojmir.

"Everyone says it's funny, because it's so alphabetical."

Gojmir looks at the hands on the clock and at the lobby, which is beginning to empty out.

"Is your brother out there making a fuss as well?" he asks.

"Yes," she says, "most of all."

"They haven't dragged him off?" Gojmir asked in a worried voice.

"Him?" Ada laughs. "Not him."

Ada really knows how to laugh; she has long black hair, that Ada, Anselmo's sister, and she's really beautiful.

The Second Photograph—
The Man in the Uniform of an Unknown Army

The photograph on which the photographer who brought the old lady a glass of water and thereby missed a good shot of the fleeing demonstrators is trying to recognize the uniform of the second of the *desaparecidos* was taken on the other side of the world, some six thousand miles from the Plaza de Mayo. It was taken by a clunky army camera, of a type German soldiers also used. It was taken in southern Austria in 1945. The grainy quality of the surface clearly indicates that it is an enlargement, and the cutoff face on one edge proves that it was cropped from a group shot. With unusual gravity, the silent eye of the camera in the officer's hands captures the faces of the soldiers at that instant. The group is sitting on the sides of a truck such that some of the young men are looking over their shoulders into the camera's eye, while others are standing in the truck bed with their hands in their pockets. And those young dry faces also look very earnest; they gaze directly into its eye as if they are absent or perhaps looking inward. Just as the officer trips the shutter, the truck coughs and shakes. Many women and children as well as the soldiers who are standing up shift anxiously. A number of shouts are heard; some wave. Then the truck starts off and people are pushed apart. The ones standing with their hands in their pockets grab the shoulders of those who are sitting. The photographer on the Plaza de Mayo could certainly not recognize the emblems on the uniform of one of the *desaparecidos* in the photograph carried by the strange old lady. That army no longer exists. That army was annihilated.

Anselmo

Their names were taken from a Spanish play, Ada explains with a laugh, while at the same time randomly pushing a pile of pamphlets and newspapers around the floor. Their father was a great admirer of Spanish drama. His particular favorite was the romantic writer José Echegaray; indeed he loved him so much that he gave them names taken from two characters in one of his plays. Gojmir, who was sitting on the side of her bed lighting a cigarette, did not find this all that funny.

"But it really is funny," Ada insisted. Don Anselmo, after whom Anselmo is named, is an old landowner. But he has an exceptionally noble heart despite all his wealth. It was this combination that my father liked, and that is why he gave Anselmo his name.

Gojmir still didn't get it.

"What is amusing," Ada says, "is that Anselmo is fighting against a good-hearted landowner. In fact Anselmo is such an important part of that fight that he has to work underground. So Anselmo is struggling against his own name, if we want to look at things symbolically."

"And Ada?" Gojmir wants to know.

"In the play Adelina is a girl in love, unhappy and doomed. Naturally she is also noble and good."

Gojmir sits on the edge of the bed and looks at Ada who is squatting on the floor amid the piles of paper and telling such amusing stories. She has a high forehead and her hair is tied back on the nape of her neck.

"I'd love to meet that Anselmo," says Gojmir.

He would meet him. Several years later we will see Gojmir, completely transformed, sitting in the same position on the edge of a bed with a just-lit cigarette, and it might well be possible to attribute that complete transformation to their having met.

Casullo

In September 1967 Gojmir suddenly found himself in Casullo, a poor suburb of Buenos Aires. With him was Anselmo, Ada's brother, who some people call Jordan. The street is muddy, the houses are low to the ground and crude, and inside one of the houses a fat, immobile woman is lying on a broken-down couch watching television. In the interval between two rain showers the sun shines on Casullo. Men are sitting on the stoops of the houses drinking the hot Paraguayan tea called maté out of dried gourds or tin cans. Dogs and cats walk across the muddy street, and crowds of curious shrieking children surround Gojmir and Anselmo. From the street they turn into an alley that is less muddy but also darker, then they cross a courtyard littered with old car tires and stop in front of a low house. A pregnant woman passes by them and greets Jordan loudly. When they enter the low house they find some young men, enveloped in a cloud of cigarette smoke.

The discussion continues unabated as the two of them sit down. It keeps going all afternoon and late into the night between heavy rain showers that plop off the roof and into the soft mud of the courtyard. In the smoky room filled with unknown glowing faces the new comrade hears political analysis and emotional speeches, he hears how people drag each other into conversation, and how the special emphasis of the oral shorthand of radical organizations cuts through the space like a sword. He hears about methods and strategies of underground activity and listens in amazement to a long speech by his friend Anselmo, who lays out his theory of the Argentine triangle whose geographic and demographic geometry determines the direction of revolutionary action. During that afternoon and the better part of the night Gojmir becomes a member of a radical political organization—whether it is called the Ejército Revolucionario Popular or something else is immaterial.

Pava, a jug filled with hot water, is passed around. They pour it over dry tea. Gojmir remembers only one name and one face. *Witold Ozynski,* with his Slavic name and fixed dry face, speaks rarely, but is sharp and decisive when he does. When he speaks he calls for deeds, less discussion but rather clear and precise action. When he takes a drag of his cigarette, he purses his lips so hard that all you see is a thin, straight line.

By the time he and Anselmo are walking across muddy Casullo, trying to light one last cigarette under an overhang before heading off to their car while each time tongues of rain put out the lighter's flame, Gojmir understands that his life has changed. In one afternoon it has so fundamentally turned that there is no going back. But you could see, Anselmo would later recall, that he was pleasantly alarmed, positively excited as Jordan would say professionally. He was inspired, ready for everything, and it was clear he had finally found some meaning in life.

El Mariscal

On November 17, 1972, a merry group is gathered in a little *capotín al paso:* Ada, Gojmir, Anselmo, and Witold. The *capotín* is packed to the gills and in the general hubbub it is hard to make out any particular conversation. The street is packed as well, filled with a crowd of people in a festive mood. The Plaza de Mayo is filled, as are the Avenidas San Martín and Santa Fe. Horns honking wildly, a river of cars floats down the Rivadavia; people are waving out the windows and enormous crowds walk along the sidewalk. Banners wave. All of Buenos Aires buzzes with great expectations. He is coming: Perón. The savior is returning after twenty years of exile. In the bar called El Mariscal the left-leaning group of friends toasts his return, the hope that he is here again. Just a few steps away, out on the street, the same illusion reigns, an illusion that has become a legend that his old comrades have brought back to life both in the wretched houses of Casullo and in the rental apartments in the center of the city; creoles, the poor and humiliated *descamisadosi* on trucks with their horns and songs amid the glittering and extravagant capital. An old myth is again becoming reality in broad daylight and before open eyes. They can't hear one another in El Mariscal because of all the noise, though they are speaking very loudly and all at once. Anselmo is singing. Gojmir watches Ada laugh and moves his glass of wine. He can catch a few syllables of Anselmo's song through the noise. It is a song about Perón that not everyone knows these days, nor is it sung on the streets, though many of them heard it in their younger days at school, over the loudspeakers. Anselmo sings about Che Guevara and winks in a friendly fashion at everyone around him. Silently, one of them observes the unusual noise, the crowds, the honking, singing, and shouting. Witold smiles calmly. But no one thinks this is unusual. They're used to him.

Letters

But, as everyone knows, that historical illusion did not last long. A myth cannot become reality. In this case it would evaporate even before the old man died (his health had been ruined by the long years of exile), leaving behind a number of parties, movements, factions, and organizations bearing his name and again leading the country to spin in a dangerous and unpredictable political whirlpool. For the friends in El Mariscal by the bubbling streets, that ecstatic moment of November 17 would, sooner or later under the force of events filled with authenticity, transform into a hallucination. El Mariscal was just a pause, a short truce in the third world war between the left and the right. In the wings and in the cellars of that glittering capital the conflict would again burst forth in all its power. The *alianza,* with its allies in the army and the police, attacked once more, initiating a new season of hunting and running, counterattacks, hiding, emigration, undercover activity. In the years that follow we see Gojmir Blagaj in that same house with the low roof in Casullo, where he has been sleeping ever more frequently; we see him talking in the warehouse of a Portuguese merchant in Mar del Plata, in the environs of Formosa with the workers on a cotton plantation, and in a middle-class apartment under chandeliers and in a leather armchair engaged in endless nighttime discussions with students in Córdoba. His mother would receive his letters filled with love and concern for her health, and they also said that everything was fine with him, and that she shouldn't worry even for a moment on his account. By her side was usually the old priest, in his dark clothes and clumsy boots with their thick soles made for some other climate, for some faraway dusty village roads that no longer exist. He would gaze silently at the strangers who brought the letters, and at her attempts, full of courteous supplication to learn something more about her son from these strangers. About his life and the strange things he was doing, about the beds he slept in, about his health and the beating of his heart. But there was no answer. The only answer and the only consolation were the letters, which she carefully saved and frequently looked at trying to discover something that would dispel her worst premonitions between the banal pleasantries and greetings to dearest mama. But her premonitions became ever more ominous, as the old priest—the gentleman, as she called him, the gentleman with the mountain boots, awkward movements, and peasantlike appearance—could, with his imperturbable perspicacity, read on her face.

The Priest

The old gentleman would tell the mother about a green glade on a wooded slope. In fact the glade was inside the forest, like a grassy gulf. It was at high elevation, and when standing there, he could see beneath his feet the entire valley with its fields, meadows, scattered houses, and a white church in the background. And at the exact moment when he would look at the church, he would see the bell ringing. The bell would swing and the clapper would crash into it with full force. Then he would wait for the sound to reach him where he stood in the glade on the wooded slope. But that never happened. The waiting would become a torment; the sky above would darken and become lower, as before a thunderstorm. And this same strange dream would repeat itself almost every night. He would always wake up, before the sound of the faraway ringing could float up to him. That is what he would say, although he knew very well that she was not listening. Everyone has his own dream and his own life. Her dreams were cut off painfully at that moment in '45 when the truck headed off to the railway station with the young man who now looks out into the room from the enlarged photograph. The priest, who had his own dream, had also been standing on that meadow and had watched the departure of that annihilated army with great anxiety, and it seemed to him that he had seen his serious face and his waving hand. But that was as far away and as long ago as the dream that woke him every night. Still, he knew that for her these were not dreams. She had never lit a candle in front of his photograph. And he also knew that it is true that where there's life there's hope. And he could not and would not take away that hope. But he felt anxious dismay welling up in his breast when he watched her ever more frequently with each passing day flipping through the letters that the various strangers brought her, watched her become ever more silent as she moved between the photograph and the letters, and as the stiff premonitions took over her face. And so he spoke more about the tribulations for which we must prepare ourselves, about grace in the face of troubles and about endurance, and ever more frequently he sensed that what was happening in this room went beyond his powers. Her ever more frantic face and his strange dreams, that photograph and that distant woodland glade, were all but a distant echo of other events, the margins of some horrible game he could no longer understand.

Black Hair

One late but still sunny February afternoon in 1974 Ada was returning home along the suburban street from school with the shouting of children still in her ears and her body a jumble of nerves when, out of the corner of her eye, she saw a big car pull away from the curb and begin to drive slowly along. Ada automatically moved to the other edge of the sidewalk. The car honked its horn loudly, and when Ada looked around she saw in the front seat a man with black hair and sideburns whose features looked somehow familiar. After taking a few more steps, she started and looked around again. Now she could also see the driver. Her brother, Anselmo, was behind the wheel, laughing uproariously. The dark-haired man was also laughing, and Ada immediately felt a strange shiver all over. It was Gojmir, her beloved, with dyed hair and a long mustache. The mustache was also dyed since; had it remained red, it would not have gone very convincingly with black hair, as she was told a little bit later. But what had scared her, literally scared her, said Ada, was the uncanny way that in that instant memory and recognition, otherness and incomprehension, had mingled together, and that instant had bewildered her to such an extent that an unknown and electric feeling had coursed from her head through her entire body. And she couldn't rid herself of that unusual sensation even after Anselmo, having invented some reason to go away, had left them alone in the car on the deserted street and Gojmir was kissing her hair and neck and lips. That evening, in the oppressive time between day and night when they were lying together on the tumbledown couch in the little house on the narrow street in Casullo, when they were listening to the growing evening murmurs of people and animals, Ada suddenly became aware of why this sensation would just not leave her: Gojmir had really changed. It was not only his appearance. Ada could clearly sense that he was exhausted, that he had aged in the year they had been apart. In the course of his work, the endless nighttime conversations, the nights spent in random safe houses, the long journeys, hiding, and agitation, he had really become a different person; he had become a professional who no longer wished to speak about his work, about the dangers he had to face, and about the ultimate goal, which was endlessly distant and perhaps unachievable. So even while she laughed as only she, with her white teeth, could laugh, and even as she looked up at his face, which was bending down toward her with closed eyes searching for her lips, Ada knew absolutely that something that had once been in him and something they had had together could never be recaptured. But she laughed; the heavier the feeling in her heart the more she laughed.

In the days that followed, Anselmo told her that something had happened to Gojmir. His organizational talent had ebbed; the calm voice and clear argumentation that had always distinguished his speech had turned into unconvincing and hesitant stuttering. Several times while out in the field among cold-storage workers he had lost it. At one nighttime meeting with radical students his surprising silence had created a terribly uncomfortable situation, and then, when he had tried to get control of the situation, his speech was so muddled that he had evoked peals of laughter. The organization was convinced that in this temporarily difficult time he needed to be put on ice for a while. This was all the more necessary because of the actions of the police and the *alianza,* which had clearly placed some well-hidden agents in their midst. A large number of their people as well as sympathizers in Buenos Aires had disappeared recently, not merely underground agents but also well-known public figures. Under these circumstances any demoralized comrade could cause a catastrophe.

The Trap

Some days later Anselmo rented a small and convenient apartment for Gojmir near the Avenida Triumvirato. Ada came to see him there regularly. She stayed by his side whenever she had time off from school. And she saw to her surprise that Gojmir was really acting ill. Like an ill man he needed her close by, needed her physical proximity, her constant touch, and the embraces that became ever more burdensome for her. Through careful questioning Ada tried to find out whether something specific had happened or whether circumstances had unexpectedly changed, just as unexpected circumstances had brought him into their midst in the first place. But eventually she realized that nothing special had happened. The disease was worse: Gojmir had lost his faith in the purpose of what he had begun. He tried to hide this from her brother, whose loud laughter and jokes sometimes brought a certain life to the sickroom. More and more frequently Gojmir spoke about his mother; he wanted to see her. He talked straightforwardly about this desire during one of Anselmo's visits. Anselmo deftly deflected the idea. When he explained that the pressure on them was ever greater and that it was more than likely that they were waiting for him there, Gojmir calmed down and wrote another long letter. One evening, when Ada was going to her parents' house, he would not let her go. "I can't take it anymore," he said.

"What can't you take, the loneliness?"

Not the loneliness, not just the loneliness. Not just the prison in which he found himself, he just couldn't take it altogether. He was an alien among them. Ada did not understand. "An alien," Gojmir shouted. He was thirty years old, an alien in their midst and nothing made any sense. That night again Ada put off her visit to her parents, something she had been doing ever since they had locked themselves up in this apartment. Then she patiently listened as he spoke calmly and for a long time in his Slavic, in his Slovene language. They stayed awake for almost the entire night, and when she tore herself away from him the next morning, some of his words went with her.

"I feel that I am in some kind of a trap here," said Gojmir. Every time she left he had the sensation that he was in some kind of a trap from which he would never escape. This Ada understood; she understood it so well that everything became clear to her: he was afraid. She didn't understand the part about being an alien. After all, he had been with them for years, he'd left his old friends and acquaintances behind long ago, and now she was with him and her brother was nearby and they were all inside the invisible but safely closed circle of their comrades. But she understood the fear. Because the truth about the ever more frequent disappearances from their ranks was no longer a secret. The organization was collapsing. And Anselmo's visits became ever more infrequent. Ada tried to suppress the feeling of pity that rose up in her alongside the feeling of disgust whenever she looked at this aged young man with the changed face and the black hair. As it grew in again, the black, dyed hair was getting light colored at the roots so that he looked as if he had a bright spot around his head. And she sometimes had a hard time hiding the oppressive heaviness with which he infected her, and in the depths of the night they would both have the feeling that something was about to happen. His fear was deep; it shot through his whole body, his heart, and his mind, which Ada no longer recognized.

Witold

When in the months that followed Anselmo searched indefatigably for his calm, pale face, he discovered that there were two versions of the circumstances that led Witold Ozynski into the midst of the pitiless compilers of blacklists and collaborators in abductions. His biography inside the organization was clear and straightforward. Sometime in '53 he had joined the student group FUBA and had taken part in its meetings and demonstrations. When FUBA was banned he was kicked out of the university, and in the years that followed, he worked in narrow circles linked to the proletariat. He did his military service, and then enrolled again in business school. During the years of civilian government he worked openly as a party official. After the blow of '67 he again went underground for the next few months or even for a whole year, at least according to the first version that Anselmo brought to light through deduction and long conversations with Witold's illegal coconspirators. According to that first version Witold became a victim of the classical method of police work, the so-called peanut man. One evening Witold is stopped by a police patrol. During a routine search of his car they discover a box of arms. That would have been sufficient to guarantee that Witold would never again see his father, never hear the Polish singing he loved so much. And now the peanut man appears. He does not let them take Witold down to a cellar where his head would be split open. Nor does he allow his teeth to be knocked out in some office. No one is allowed to touch him at all. His famous sixth sense about people leads him to guess that he can try something else this time. The weapons go back in the glove compartment. Witold drives around town for an entire night, completely confused, his heart beating rapidly and the blood boiling in his temples. After two hours of continuous driving he realizes that no one is following him. He decides to keep quiet about his encounter with the police. Because how would he prove that they had let him go for no reason. And Witold is well aware of what happens to people in his circle who are allowed to go for no reason. He leaves the weapons at the appointed spot. In the days that follow he never leaves his father's store. Every time a stranger rings the bell and enters the door he feels a sick emptiness in the pit of his stomach, as if he is on a roller coaster. After some ten days of fear, nervous days, and ominous sleepless nights, he greets the little man as a kind of savior. In the back room of his father's office the visitor asks for some kind of dish or plate on which he can put peanut shells. The visits and long nighttime conversations keep on for a time. And then Witold comes back to them.

Anselmo got this version from his comrades, who had built it on a long thread of data. But there was something missing here. This classical method of softening up was too simple. It did not seem to jibe with Witold's pale face and his pursed lips, the calm and decisive face that Anselmo had seen countless times with his own eyes when he was waiting in empty streets or when he came upon him in a dark foyer. It is not the time to be occupied with Anselmo's reconstruction of the second version while Gojmir is sitting on the bed, totally ready, and waiting for someone to set him on his way. But you have to imagine Anselmo walking for many hours through the capital's streets with Witold's former fiancée, a girl who understood nothing, pumping her for all the details she knew about this strange, passionate, and pale man, how he and his father conversed in the little office behind the store, until she moved away to some unknown place, but you have to realize that Anselmo's road to the second version was long and difficult and outside his experience. Anselmo senses that the second version is obscure. The second version insists that Witold had gone over to the other side from the very beginning.

In the beginning there was a moment in Witold's youth, one afternoon in '44 when in the Ozynski apartment the astonished and worried family was looking at a newspaper whose large-type headline printed the name of a strange place: Katyn Forest. In the paper filled with official German propaganda, there is a large photograph. An open grave, a pit full of corpses. The horror that filled Witold's young soul that night passed through the Ozynski apartment like a terrifying chasm. His head spun with enormous, unknown things. He couldn't sleep all night, and from the kitchen he could hear someone sobbing and crying out for vengeance. It seemed to him that those cries filled the chasm he felt in his chest, the chasm in the heavy space around his heart.

According to the second version—which is confirmed not so much by the facts of his work but rather by his face, his behavior at the meetings in Casullo, his unexpected absence in the *capotín al paso,* and his pursed lips—according to that version Witold had been on the other side and in secret contact from the very beginning.

Anselmo will never know which of the two versions is correct. But is it really important? Even if the first of Anselmo's viewpoints is *classical* and the other is *obscure,* or even if we see them both together as a tangled net of *accidents,* it is in any case clear that fate brought Witold and Gojmir Blagaj together. It could have been someone else who cut through his life with the sharp ring of the doorbell in the night. But the person who came late at night and rang at Gojmir's door was none other than Witold. Probably he was fated to do that from the very beginning, according to the first version, the second version, or in spite of both.

The Ring in the Night

When the sound of the doorbell cut into the space between their four walls, Gojmir started and went pale. As if suspecting something, he got up off the bed and then sat down on it. Ada would later say that all day long there had been something in his behavior that had been weighing heavily on him with mysterious power. Perhaps it only seems that way to her now, perhaps everything happened quite differently. For she couldn't let herself be completely carried away by her memories. She couldn't remember, for example, what film she had been watching when the bell rang. For a time she was sure that it was an Italian film in which Marcello Mastroianni, quiet and forlorn, was saying something to some famous actress. Now it seems to her that it wasn't that, now she is sure there was shouting and shooting, but she knows for sure that she turned down the volume before she went over to the door.

When the sound of the bell unexpectedly cut through their four walls, Gojmir was sitting on the bed. Ada, who was sitting on an armchair in front of the television with her legs curled up underneath her, stood up, pulled the thin fabric of the nightgown that had ridden up around her thighs down to her knees, threw a skirt over it, and went to the door.

"Hang on," Gojmir said. "You don't know who it is."

"Anselmo, who else?" said Ada.

But it was not Anselmo standing at the door, it was Witold Ozynski.

"It's Witold," Ada said. "He wants you."

"Why doesn't he come in?" said Gojmir.

"He's going to wait in the car," said Ada, "and you will go with them." She stood in the middle of the room staring fixedly at him. Today she says at that moment she knew something was about to happen. But Witold, Witold, Witold—there simply couldn't be anything wrong. And there was precisely something in Gojmir's gaze that was searching for something in her eyes, precisely Witold was in his gaze. She stood and watched as he got dressed. He buttoned his light-colored shirt very slowly, and then it took him such a long time to get his arms through the sleeves of his jacket that they could hear a nervous honking from down below on the street.

"It's annoying," said Gojmir, "but I'll go anyway."

But, says Ada, his voice sounded like he was trying to suppress a terrible internal tension. He said it on purpose to divert her attention from his eyes, which raced around the four walls of the room as if trying to cling to something there. Then he reached into his pocket and clasped his watch in his palm as if he always carried it that way. Now Ada realizes that his hands were shaking and that the watch slipped through his fingers twice as he tried to clasp it. But Ada only saw things that way much later, when she was recounting them to Anselmo and his comrades or when she was trying to explain things as delicately as possible to the old lady with the two photographs. The old lady did not listen to her. In fact she could not listen to anyone. She could see other things and she could see into depths that Ada could not perceive, even if Ada remembered every single detail.

Gojmir stood in the middle of the room and fiddled in his pockets. Again the nervous honking came from down below. Gojmir stepped over to Ada and patted her elbow with the back of his hand.

"I'll be back soon," he said.

But he never came back.

The Transport

When in May 1945 the truck got to the little railroad station, many soldiers climbed into the open cattle cars. The young man from the photograph jumped over the edge of the truck bed. British soldiers stood around the station and the train. By the side of his jeep an officer was talking with a railway man and nervously slapping a stick against his breeches. The loading was taking place continuously, although without the noise, shouting, and rushing about typical for military transports. Together with many bodies in gray uniforms the young man from the photograph pushed his way toward the passenger car that was hitched just behind the locomotive. A group of officers from his army was standing next to it in a semicircle, and they were quietly listening to the tramp of army boots in the wagons. The young man from the photograph waved his hand nervously and said something to one of the officers in the semicircle. They waved their hands and turned away. The young man moved away from them and glanced back to where his officers were climbing into the passenger car. Someone from the open maw of the nearest car reached out his hand. Grabbing the proffered right hand with both of his the young man jumped up. A minute later he could hear the clanging of the doors, which the English soldiers suddenly pushed closed along their narrow tracks. The young man from the photograph leaned against the thick wooden side of the door and looked around. Everyone was pale and quiet. Everyone was silent. From the outside of the wagon they could hear the metallic clack of the bolts being slid into the hasps. Then the train moved. A few seconds later footsteps were heard on the roof. Up above someone laughed loudly.

"Jesus," said the boy standing next to the young man from the photograph, the same boy who had held out his hand to help him climb into the wagon.

"Jesus," he said, and he looked at him with wavering eyes.

And then he added quietly:

"Blagaj, where are they taking us?"

The Journey

In the front seat was a stocky driver whom Gojmir did not recognize. Witold was sitting in the backseat, his hands on his knees, and he was looking directly in front of him at the road, which was becoming more and more empty. Witold's immobility suddenly became unbearable.

"Witold," Gojmir said, "where are we going?"

Witold remained silent.

"Witold," Gojmir said loudly and decisively, "this is not the road to Casullo."

Witold did not answer; the driver shook his head and looked in the rearview mirror. The enormous old Buick raced through the dark and empty suburban streets. The houses became fewer and farther apart. Then the headlights raked a low building and as the driver turned he honked loudly twice. Just as they stopped, an unknown man appeared in the headlight's beam, and another man opened the door on the side where Gojmir was sitting. He threw himself down on the seat next to him without a word, while the one in front of the car disappeared from the illuminated circle and a moment later sat down in the front seat. The Buick took off with a start as soon as the person in the front found the door and then shut it with a bang. The silent company raced along the long rural road into the night.

The man on his left stank of vodka. On his right Gojmir could feel the heat of Witold's body. The man on his left was shoving him into him. Gojmir leaned forward and looked straight into Witold's face. His eyes were staring fixedly at the road that was being raked by the car's headlights. Gojmir ran his eyes over Witold's masklike face.

"Witold," Gojmir said in a dry and low voice, "what does this mean?"

His words hung in the air, shook in the air, and then flapped like frightened birds around the dark masculine heads in the car. Then they disappeared, swallowed by the monotonous hum of the car's engine. In the car it was dark and quiet.

The Station

The moment the train stopped, cudgels and rifle butts banged against the sides of the car. Many malevolent people surged around the wagon. The voices of men and women demanded death to the traitors. The men in the cattle car tried to escape from the battering like a frightened herd of sheep. Someone tried to pray. Someone said, "This is the end."

But it was not the end. It was the beginning of the end.

Blagaj could sense that the boy next to him was searching for his hand. He squeezed it weakly; it was wet and cold.

The Brickworks

The car flies over the potholed asphalt road. It is dark. The lights of the city have been left far behind. Then the headlights shine onto a long, low building surrounded by piles of broken bricks that crunch under the car's tires. The three men get out and pull Gojmir from the car. The driver cuts the engine and leans over the wheel. No voice, no wind. The air is still, like immobile matter, as the group heads toward a large clay pit near the brickworks.

A Different Pit

In that long-ago year of 1945, at the other end of the world, some six thousand miles away from the abandoned brickworks and the clay pit toward which three men are leading Gojmir Blagaj with his dyed hair and transformed appearance, a column of men wearing torn and rumpled uniforms, surrounded by armed guards, stops by the side of a forested road near the town of Kočevje. Three men unwind a strand of telephone wire from a big drum and snip it with wire cutters. The guards take the pieces of wire and tie the prisoners' hands behind their backs. The sounds of individual gunshots and volleys of machine-gun fire ring out nearby. Eyes wandering, the prisoner from the column, whom we will recognize later on the grainy enlargement cut from a group photograph on the Plaza de Mayo, watches the guard's hands, which are tying his wrists tightly with the wire. Then he gazes into his eyes, bloodshot from sleepless nights on guard duty.

"Please," he suddenly whispers, "tie them loosely."

The guard looks at him in amazement.

"I have a son," he says, "please."

"I can't," says the guard and he looks around. "I can't."

"His name is Gojmir," the prisoner says loudly, so that the quiet and pale men all around him get anxious, like a frightened herd of sheep.

"What's going on there?" shouts a voice from the edge of the forest. The guard steps back and shoves his rifle butt in the prisoner's back.

The column moves on. The shots are ever closer.

There is a deep pit.

The Abyss

At the beginning of the 1980s, the entire world learned about the mass graves that were discovered near Campo de Mayo, in the La Plata cemetery and in a number of other places. The papers began to publish all the details, and the television networks showed pictures of despairing mothers on the Plaza de Mayo who were demanding their sons, or at least their bodies. Ever more victims of an insane underground war that had brought victory to no one were exhumed from the pits. The only thing that remained in its wake were human lives buried in pits and long lists of *desaparecidos* who had vanished to God knows where. Some caudillo who had supposedly killed them with his own hands was put on trial, but the man remained silent during his court appearance. What else could he do? He could not return sons to their mothers. Some people who had managed to run away from the shots in the dark of night were also located. They also remained silent. There was just one Creole who was said to have climbed out of a pit full of corpses and who would talk about what he saw there for a glass of whiskey. He said he had been taken to the edge of a precipice with his hands bound. The man who went with him shot him in the back of the head with a revolver. But the bullet had only grazed his ear and he fell alive into the pit. He fell onto corpses and in the pit there was a terrible sighing, moaning, and crying, for many were still alive. In the middle of the night he had dragged himself out into the open through a badly filled section and run away. But that was just a story that circulated among people. No one could verify it because the drunken Creole had soon disappeared somewhere in the interior of the country and vanished into the broad pampas. And those *desaparecidos,* so to speak, who had again appeared among the populace, remained solemn and silent.

The Cave of Trophonius

The ancient Greeks said of gloomy and mournful people that they had visited the cave of Trophonius. Whoever had seen its terrors, the underground passages and serpents, and whoever had escaped from it bore a dark shadow on his face for the rest of his life.

Probably the real Trophonius was the person who, together with his brother, built Apollo's famous temple at Delphi. As the brothers were known to be great architects, the powerful king Hyrieus asked them to build a special, well-guarded structure in which he could hide his treasure. The brothers soon built it, but they also built a hidden entrance to it with an eye to stealing the riches. Hyrieus had feared something of the kind and created a trap. But he only caught Agamedes. Trophonius tried to get his brother out of the trap several times. When he realized he would not be able to free him and that he himself would not be able to hide because he could be recognized by the facial traits he shared with his brother, he cut off his brother's head and took it away with him. At that moment the earth opened and swallowed him up.

One had to go to a cave at the edge of a forest. Those who were brave enough could go into it to find something hidden or a prophecy. But they could ask for advice only after having endured terrible trials. Not everyone could do it; not everyone returned. The only way to the entrance of the cavern, which yawned like a black maw, was through a long series of underground passages and rooms. Then one had to descend a staircase, which led to the final hole. This had such a narrow opening that one first had to stick his legs in and could only get his body to go through by squeezing very hard. This was followed by a quick and steep fall to the bottom of the cave. Anyone who wanted to hear a prophecy or receive counsel had to go the whole way while carrying a honey cake in his hands. This was used to calm the serpents that swarmed and squirmed all over the cavern. Simultaneously you could not touch the invisible machinery that would eventually push you out of the pit. You could spend an entire day and night in the terrible bottom of the pit. Some people never returned. Some had the good fortune to hear a prophecy. With the help of the aforementioned invisible machinery, they were then able to get back to the surface, but in such a way that their legs came out first while their head hung down below. Outside they would then sit on a chair called *Mnemozina,* the goddess of memory, and they would recall the terrible impressions from the cave, which were burnt into their minds for the rest of their life.

Epilogue

But we need to bring this story to a close. The three men lead Gojmir toward the abandoned brickworks. He doesn't ask anything more, nor is he thinking about escaping. He searches Witold's immobile face for some kind of strange misunderstanding that will now be explained. But the presence of the two guys walking right next to him and the third who remains leaning over the steering wheel tells him that this will not happen. It will also not happen because Witold, the avenger of some old pit, is walking behind him with pursed lips. Nor does it help to know that Gojmir has no connection of any kind with that pit. He is entwined in a terrible and senseless game, and, his hair dyed, he walks along the long, dark building toward the end of the path with ever-diminishing hope in his heart.

We will leave them on the path—and not because we want to avoid the kinds of details that are published in the papers and in the survivors' accounts. We will leave them in deference to Ada and her hopes. In the days that followed she would be seized with anxiety and then by a terrible premonition. She was suddenly sorry for every harsh word she had uttered, for every evil thought. Perhaps she even felt bad about the afternoon that she ran from the street into a bank carrying a stack of books and met a boy who no longer exists. She would search for him in Casullo and around the cold-storage lockers hoping to find him among the workers carrying a pile of newspapers under his arm, with his light or dark hair. Then she would go to visit his mother and sit silently in front of her two photographs. We will also leave them in deference to Anselmo who under the name of Jordan, pistol in his pocket, would open the doors of offices and ring the bell of middle-class apartments trying to see Witold's calm face and his pursed lips. Once he would hear that he had been sighted in Rosario at a police parade on the May 25 jacaranda festival. He went with a group of comrades to search for him there, but they did not find him. And that was just as well, because otherwise the most senseless of all wars in the history of mankind, the third world war of ideologies, would have claimed another victim. And we will leave them in deference to the old lady who walks around the Plaza de Mayo with the photographs of two *desaparecidos* in the great and crazy hope that she will never have to light a candle in front of their pictures. Some of the permanent visitors to the Plaza de Mayo know her. The photographer who is there with his camera at the ready to snap some exceptionally important event laughs pleasantly at her. It would never occur to him to snap her, whose steadfast hope and faith is the greatest, most miraculous event. Some of those who walk the square also recognize the old village priest who comes across the smooth surface of the square in his clumsy boots, takes the old lady under the arm, and then walks off with her past the statue of Pedro de Mendoza.

▪ ▫ ▪ ▫ ▪

A TALE ABOUT EYES

WE HAVE BEFORE US TWO STORIES CONCERNING THE OVERWHELMING impression produced in a person when he looked into the eyes of a man he admired.

The first is the account of Kurt Erich Suckert, who when he meets Ante Pavelić is bathed in a clear and natural ray of light, reminiscent of the best impressionist canvases: "At first glance I saw only the bright gleam of his eyes, like the shimmer of a river's surface."

The second is that of Henry Abrams, whose ophthalmologist's subtle knowledge is overwhelmed by an inability to suppress a certain quavering, practically divine realization as he recalls a glance into the blue eyes of Albert Einstein: "His eyes were angelic. You had the feeling that they knew everything in the world."

We have before us two scenes.

In the first, the object of interest is a bowl on a desk. The bowl is filled with some kind of small, spherical fruit. In the dim light they look like grapes or currants, but they aren't grapes or currants. The office is so small that the visitor has to sit with his back practically against the door. Behind the desk, which occupies almost half the room, sits a man in a uniform. The two sit eye to eye, as it were. Green light, the reflection of green trees on the hillside, filters through a window that looks out onto a square. The cramped room seems even smaller than it is because of the languid movements and warm serious voice of the man behind the desk in whose eyes the visitor can see the shimmer of a green river. The man takes the bowl in his hands and pushes it across the polished surface of the desk. The visitor, who had initially thought that the bowl contained some kind of fruit, grapes or currants, now realizes with a horror that threatens to overcome him that the spheres in the bowl are human eyes, gouged or cut out of their sockets. The year is 1942 and the visitor is Kurt Erich Suckert. Some two years later, even before the end of the war, his description of this scene (published under his pen name Curzio Malaparte) will become one of the blackest legends of our century. The story will find its way into other literary texts and, eventually, into histories. The office, the hands, the bowl filled with human eyes—all of these belong to the man in the uniform: Ante Pavelić. Everyone finds the scene convincing. No one doubts its truth, an illustration of Pavelić's horrifying proclivity to collect human eyes.

In the second scene we see hands that pick up a jelly jar and raise it to eye level. The jar is filled with colorless liquid, probably formaldehyde, and on the bottom are two small spheres. The hands shake the jar and the spheres move. They shake it again and the spheres turn and slowly rotate in the embrace of the jellylike substance, then come to rest again. The hands carefully place the jar back on the table and the eyeballs sink to the bottom. Now they are facing up and they gaze motionlessly at the man who had shaken them, right up close. The person stares at them dreamily. The scene occurs in complete silence, broken only by the sound of cars on the road. He glances fixedly at the eyes that rest faceup on the bottom of the jar, and they glance back at him. The jar contains a pair of human eyes. The room in which this silent confrontation takes place is neither a morgue nor the laboratory of some clinic. It is an apartment in a small vacation home in a godforsaken town somewhere on the East Coast in New Jersey. The year is 1994, and the apartment, the hands, the jelly jar, and the eyes inside it are all the property of a man named Henry Abrams. The eyes that stare up motionlessly at the owner of the jelly jar are those of Albert Einstein. At the end of December of that year a picture of the jar and the eyeballs will be beamed all over the world. But few will believe it; the scene will be considered an invention, an oculist's bizarre fantasy.

What is true in the first scene is the description of the leader's office, the surroundings of Zagreb's Upper Town. True also is the description of the movements, voice, and eyes of the man in the uniform, if the shimmer of the green river in his eyes can be considered the truth. But Malaparte is a writer, and his truth is different. In an article he would write in the same year as his meeting with Pavelić (published in the Italian newspaper *Documento*), the sentences would radiate clever literary admiration: Ante Pavelić on the threshold of the office, tall, thin, with the gray reflection of the cold light of dawn on his face. "At first glance I saw only the clear reflection of his eyes," Malaparte writes, "the shimmer of a river's surface." Even the environment in which the leader lived and ruled is described through the shining of human eyes. "The environs of Zagreb are full of music," he writes, "an architecture of green tones (green is the deepest color). The presence of the Sava River gives nature an undertone of blue, a tender and firm glimmer. Something like the glint of human eyes." Curzio Malaparte admires the leader's decisive manner, his unpretentious way of speaking, his modesty. He writes about Pavelić's red cheeks, his muscular body, fleshy lips full of proud will, and again, about his deep eyes.

The writer accompanied the leader on a trip to Monfalcone, and when they paused on the road between Ljubljana and Postojna, they saw a peasant couple working a patch of land amid the rocks of the Karst. Pavelić speaks about the land, and Malaparte strives to remember every word. His love for the land is connected to "its tranquil, good, noble, and chaste dignity" he would write. "I began to understand," he writes, "that the mystery of Ante Pavelić is a mystery of extraordinary nobility, and that the land itself is mysterious, perhaps even more so than flesh and blood." Malaparte admires Pavelić.

At around the same time, at the other end of the world, the face of a great thinker was being observed by his private physician. During his eye exam, Einstein jokes, he teaches his young friend lessons about life. The young doctor, Henry Abrams, who is mentioned only in passing by Einstein's biographers as one among a number of intellectual friends, was the guardian of Einstein's health between 1939 and 1941. Guardian is a poor choice of words, however, for their relations really went in the opposite direction. Einstein was the guardian and Abrams his ward. Relations between guardian and ward were marked by boundless admiration. Each time Einstein looked at him, the young Abrams felt shivers down his spine. The eyes into which he glanced contained an entire universe of wisdom and knowledge. "His eyes," he would say years later, "were angelic. You had the impression that they knew everything in the world." It was in fact Einstein who pushed the young doctor to specialize exclusively in ophthalmology. After the war Abrams did so, and several years later, now an eye specialist, he found himself at the same university, Princeton, in the same place as Einstein. Their friendship blossomed again in its original form. Abrams would visit the object of his admiration at home, where the two would talk for hours about everything except students. The guardian did his best to hook his ward up with a girl. And once a year Einstein would come to Dr. Abrams's office for an eye exam. Here, too, there was no lack of admiration. "His eyes," Abrams would later say, "were as clear as crystal, they were endlessly deep."

In 1944, with a sudden and unexpected gesture of a type that was not uncommon in his life, Curzio Malaparte repudiated Ante Pavelić. The gesture in itself was not surprising, for the leader's hour was passing and Suckert's political allegiances were shifting. What was surprising was its violence. He repudiated Pavelić with a violence more characteristic of a rejected lover from a land that may be more mysterious than flesh and blood. In his book *Kaputt* he describes Ante Pavelić as a cold-blooded criminal and sadist, a remarkable turnabout for this writer. And so he needed a huge, deep, fleshy, earthy, bloody metaphor with which to replace the shining eyes that glimmered like a river's surface. Where before there were shining eyes, now there are the horribly gouged-out, the horribly peaceful and silent gouged-out, eyes of Serbs and Jews from concentration camps in the bowl on the desk, disembodied eyes that looked out into the dark silence of the office, eyes that would never again see green rivers and the architecture of dark green tones—green that is the deepest color. And the notorious horrifying bowl on Pavelić's desk would feed the imagination of historians, writers, and biographers. Whole generations would understand it as a metaphor for Ustaša crimes, and it would captivate their imagination as an example of the incomprehensible mystery of evil, which contains more mystery than flesh and blood, perhaps more mystery than the earth itself. Men of the pen and the mind would appear, and they would claim that they, too, with their own eyes as it were, had seen the bowl filled with gouged-out eyeballs that from a distance looked a bit like some kind of fruit, although they were really human eyes that had been torn out by bayonets. Malaparte's bowl of eyes on Pavelić's desk would leave an immutable stamp on this century of evils, a judgment against that world and a judgment against the time of the *quator hominum novissima*—death, judgment, hell, and heaven. It would make no difference that Raffaele Casertano, an Italian diplomat who was present during the conversation between the writer and the leader, denied the existence of the bowl. Equally useless would be the commentary of some sober individuals who would say that, given the quantity of proof of the Ustaša's actual crimes, there is no need to invent anything. Malaparte is deep and mysterious. He sees the bowl filled with gouged-out eyes, and everyone else sees it clearly through his eyes.

When Dr. Abrams heard that Albert Einstein had died, his life was transformed in an instant. The world in which he lived in close proximity to a person he worshipped had been destroyed. In fact, in his own words, it seemed that the world had ceased rotating: "I felt that the world had stopped." Later he would say that it was a stroke of luck that brought him to Princeton Hospital at that exact moment. Without having thought it through, he knew what he had to do—to save those eyes, the clearest crystal, the deepest and wisest. The whole thing took little more than twenty minutes. "I needed only scissors and tweezers," he would say forty years later. That very night in the morgue Einstein's young friend first cut the optic nerve and sliced through the six connecting muscles. Very far back, he would say, so as not to damage the eyeball. Then he removed Einstein's eyes from their sockets with the tweezers and put them in a glass bottle. He poured liquid over them to prevent these treasures that would now belong to him from drying out. Later he would transfer the eyes to a different jar, and eyewitnesses would say that it was indeed a jelly jar. And he would hide it in his home for the next forty years. When in December 1994 he made the true story public, fearing in his old age that his secret might go with him to the grave, no one wanted to believe him.

Abrams was a man of reason, and it was his devotion to reason that led him to the same type of action that motivated people in the Middle Ages when they cut the limbs off saints, believing in their eternal divine power. Likewise, he thought it reasonable to save the eyes which contained all the wisdom of the world.

Some years after the war, a Croatian writer recalled how during the war he happened to be invited to visit the headquarters of the Croatian government. He remembered, as if it was happening today before his very eyes, what occurred when by mistake he walked through an unlocked door in the leader's quarters. There he saw something that made his blood freeze: on the desk was a bowl filled with eyeballs. When people who worked there at the time told him that he could not have seen anything of the sort, he angrily rebuked them. He hadn't just read about this but had seen it with his completely healthy eyes, and he was, at that time just as today, in full possession of his faculties. The Slovene writer Vitomil Zupan, or at least his first-person Partisan hero, saw those eyes even earlier, immediately after the Ustaša had cut them out of their sockets. He sees them near a tiny village named Ogulin, from which they are to be sent to Zagreb, and writes about them in a short story titled "Blue Eyes for Pavelić" that was published shortly after the war. An icy-cold wind is blowing through the hills around Ogulin, where a Partisan patrol lies in ambush. The young hero thinks about the cigarettes that he will find in the pockets of the dead enemies, hoping for, as Zupan writes, "a comb made of bone, thin and long, with which he would comb his wet mane into a beautiful coif, as if in the city." After a tense wait, two passersby appear with the letter *U* on their caps. The Partisans kill the first one on the spot, but the other, "a real ox," is only wounded. A wild chase after the escaping beast ensues. Grenades litter the snow, the man is wounded, and he leaves a pool of blood with each step. Eventually he drops, riddled with bullets. In disgust the Partisan looks at the flat, pocked face with its pancake nose and its open, round eye. He rifles through the pockets and finds a photograph showing the Ustaša holding a knife between his teeth; the knife is painted blood red. Then he opens the man's knapsack. "Inside were some three hundred and forty pairs of human eyes. The blue eyes were in a separate little bag." On the bag the Ustaša, "that ox," had written "in colored pencil: blue eyes for Pavelić (girls')."

The Croatian writer's story and that of Vitomil Zupan serve as confirmation of Malaparte's description. And, more recently, chronicles and historical works have included it.

At the beginning of 1955, Albert Einstein began to suffer ever more severely from what is called an abdominal aneurysm. On Saturday, April 16, 1955, he began to complain of sharp pain all over his body. The pain was so strong that he passed out in his bathroom. He was taken to Princeton Hospital. His young friend Henry Abrams happened to be right by him at that time. There was no longer any possibility of looking into those crystal eyes and their vivid depths. The eyes were fading. Einstein's son was the last person to speak with him. They talked about politics and made some corrections to his last project, the unified field theory. On Monday, at 1:15 in the morning, Einstein mumbled his last words. No one knows what he said. He spoke them to the nurse in German, and although she was of course listening carefully, she did not know a word of that language. When the ophthalmologist Abrams heard that his terrestrial god had died, it only took him an instant to decide to save those beloved eyes for humanity. At around four in the morning he went to the morgue, and there, with the specialized knowledge of an eye doctor, he was able to complete the job in some twenty minutes. In a sense the New Jersey oculist felt that his twenty-minute act was a major feat. He gave Albert Einstein eternal life. "I felt," he said later, "that he could not die, that his eyes stood for all of his influence." Because they had been preserved, Abrams thought that the great man would now live forever. From time to time he thought of dissecting them, but the divine shiver that passed through him whenever he glanced at them caused him to change his mind. When he would finally show them to amazed reporters in 1994 he would say ecstatically: "You see, they look like new." A friend of Einstein asserts that the father of relativity frequently said that he wanted to be cremated so that after his death people would not be able to come and rummage among his bones. And that is what was done. After a modest eulogy attended by only a dozen or so mourners, the old man's ashes were scattered, just as he had wished—no one knows exactly where but probably over the Delaware River. The mourners who were followed by his glance (which slid over the surface of the river) would probably have been robbed of the tranquilizing vision of ephemerality had they known that his eyes, the instrument and vessel of his glance, had been hidden in a jelly jar.

After the war, during a talk in Athens, Malaparte admitted that the story about the bowl filled with gouged-out human eyes on Pavelić's desk was an invention. When he was asked why he had made it up, he laughed quickly and added: "It's all the same whether they were human eyes or grapes or currants. I wanted to achieve an effect, and you can't feed the imagination on currants." The astonished silence that ensued proves only that the imagination had indeed fed on those currants, and that the imagination had already turned them into the actual dead eyes of our century; eyes that, with their silent glance, also speak about the living eyes of Ante Pavelić with the shimmer of a green river, about those eyes that contained an unusual and sensitive power, as the very same author had written. Such was this power that the writer subordinated his voice to it, as it is said in the Bible: "I try to make you love me, for your eyes are over me, your servant." And such was this power that Kurt Erich Suckert, with the same mysterious, earthly passion that had once possessed him, gouged out those eyes, multiplied them, and put them in a bowl in his famous account.

And in a similar way somebody else, Henry Abrams (now an old-timer but a young man when he cut them out), possesses eyes that send divine shivers down his spine. In an apartment on the East Coast in New Jersey, the wrinkled but once-upon-a-time smooth and dexterous hands of Henry Abrams clumsily pick up and shake the jelly jar. In his opinion it contains a relic more precious than those in the cathedral of Cologne. His hands touch the glass top of the jar that contains the spheres covered with liquid and move it toward his own once flexible but now somewhat weak eyes. The spheres slowly sink to the bottom, where they come to rest side by side, and they look quietly and motionlessly at the person who finds love and knowledge in them and a great deal more besides. For, as he said, when you look into those eyes you see all the beauty and mystery of the world.

It is said that after he looks at them for a long time, he puts the eyes into a bag and takes them by car to a storage facility an hour away. He wouldn't want anything unexpected to happen to them.

That could easily be the end of the tale. And what do we really have in our hands that made it worth the telling? An old oculist who drives some eyes, carefully preserved in formaldehyde, down some empty road in New Jersey. A bowl filled with currants and Suckert's short laugh from which a fantasy grows. We have two stories and two scenes. We can only sense the link between them, but we can't fully grasp it. We suspect also that the eyes stored in the secure vault know what is happening to them. And so did the real or invented eyes in the bowl on the desk in the darkened room of that war year. That suspicion is exasperating, but a horrible allure that gives birth to further stories grows from it, although nothing is certain here. The only sure thing is that somewhere there are eyes even more angelic, eyes that know even more, whose gleam is even stronger than the green shimmer of a river's surface. And the vision of those eyes accompanies us. They alone know where the end of a tale is, and what will happen even before a reliable end is reached.

■ □ ■ □ ■

A SUNDAY IN OBERHEIM

NOT EVEN A SUNDAY, JUST A SUNDAY MORNING. THREE SCENES, A thousand words. And the necessary backdrop of the melancholy Central European provinces. The square by the Danube: the river has risen a bit in the last few days, and the long-hulled boats, either on their own or with the aid of tugboats, struggle against the current, but they slide quickly and almost soundlessly in the other direction as the brown water foams. The wind stirs the tops of the poplars, clumps of white acacias toss in the breeze, somewhere upriver it is raining, while here a dull and foggy light can be seen through the clouds. Organ music emanating from the church of St. Egidio rolls over the cobblestones, and it bounces off the houses whose empty facades look like inside-out city walls, the powerful sounds chase one another and swirl around the Gothic building. It is deserted. Everyone is at mass.

Several cars park in front of the abandoned brewery on the other side of the tiny street on which I am living. I don't know why I've never noticed before. They park here, and some men carrying elegant gun cases in their hands get out and disappear through the broad door, which must lead into a cellar or warehouse. Once upon a time they rolled beer barrels here and loaded them onto carts. The brewery tower looks over the roofs at the Danube. I'd like to be up on it, right on top. I'd be able to see where the misty rain from the low clouds meets the river in its upper reaches. Beneath the tower is a smaller, mostly abandoned building.

"It was an ice shed," Fastl explains.

Fastl isn't at mass, ever. He doesn't want me to use the formal forms of address, just "you, Fastl." He once worked for the railway. Now he keeps a hot-dog stand in the small train station. Jadranka from Bosnia cooks and sells the hot dogs. Every Sunday, when the stand is closed, Fastl goes to drink beer at the Black Eagle. You can find some others who don't go to mass there.

"They loaded ice with the beer," he explains.

"And what's in the brewery now?"

"Nothing. In 1945 just here near the entrance three people were killed by a grenade from an American tank."

Another car parks in front of the brewery. A broad-shouldered man rings the bell by the door, waits, and disappears inside.

"And where are those people going?"

"To the cellar."

"But you, Fastl, say there's nothing in the old brewery."

"Only in the cellar."

The small, brown eyes in his big head shine puckishly.

He asks whether I'd like to see what is in the cellar.

"Yeah."

"Let's go," he says.

We cross the street. Fastl rings, and a man's voice can be heard through the intercom. They speak in a dialect I don't understand. The door opens and we find ourselves on a long, stone staircase that leads down into the depths. It smells like sulfur and as if something were burning. I seem to hear a vigorous crackling, as if someone were smashing a heavy tree branch. Fastl is retired; he walks cautiously and we are illuminated by the yellow rays of the cellar light. Down below is another door. My guide rings again and it opens as well. Now we're in a small room where a tall, close-cropped man sits at a table reading a newspaper. He nods, which means we can proceed, and we suddenly find ourselves in a bigger, better-lit room.

It is full of close-cropped, broad-shouldered men, most of them wearing vests over shirts with rolled-up sleeves. Those same elegant gun cases are lying open on the table, and inside them are neatly arranged revolvers of various calibers, together with gun-cleaning supplies.

"*Schutzverein,*" says Fastl, "a gun club." Some bigger pieces are leaning against the wall—shotguns, Winchesters, some automatics. The crackling is now louder, the smell of sulfur sharper than it was upstairs. A grayish-blue cloud floats above our heads, and it hugs the high vaults of the cellar. There are no windows. The men walk out through heavy, metal-framed doors and come back in with serious faces. They handle their weapons like small animals, carefully and lightly, with practiced motions. Fastl speaks with the broad-shouldered man who just arrived. He nods. From underneath a bar covered with a forest of beer mugs someone pulls out a kind of earphones and presses them into our hands. We go through the same doors, which emit a cloud of bluish smoke every time they open.

As soon as we walk through the door we hear an explosion. A young man is holding something like a pistol, a Browning, a Luger, a kind of bazooka in his hands. Fastl and I put on the earphones; his eyes shine. Two people are shooting at a target with small-bore pistols; a young man with a bazooka is shooting at panels covered with human outlines. Some are closer, some farther away. They rise and fall, run as if scared, hide, and rush out the other side of the hall. But the bullets from the spluttering gun catch up to them there as well. The walls are covered with thick foam rubber. The shooter is satisfied, though he doesn't say anything, wordlessly giving way to the next in line. He has a long barrel, which he balances on his left elbow, aims, and shoots. Fastl points out to me that the shooter is hitting the target right on the head, in the forehead.

When we return to the first underground room, the broad-shouldered hippopotamus offers me a beer, and a close-cropped man asks Fastl to ask me whether I'd like to try. I say no. The close-cropped hippo says that I'm no Hemingway and I say that I'm not. The broad-shouldered guy asks whether I want a beer and I say no thanks. Fastl says that he will have a beer at the Black Eagle, just like he does every Sunday morning. Then the broad-shouldered guy and his close-cropped friend devote themselves to a discussion about the apparatuses in fitness clubs, while Fastl and I climb through the yellow light up the stone steps. The grayish-blue smoke clings to us, the crackling, as if someone were breaking up tree branches down below, gets farther away. It still smells of sulfur.

Outside it is Sunday morning. It is completely quiet in front of the scorched and empty bakery. The wind stirs the tops of the poplars, somewhere upriver it is raining, and here a dull and foggy light can be seen through the clouds. The brewery tower looks over the roofs at the Danube. I'd like to be up on it, right on top. I'd be able to see where the drizzly rain from the low clouds meets the river in its upper reaches. I ask what is in the brewery tower. Fastl says nothing, but if I'd like we can go see. I say no. The street is completely quiet. Nothing would indicate that people are shooting around here, I say. Lentia, the gun club is called Lentia. Fastl shrugs and cuts across the courtyard and the little garden plots on his way to the Black Eagle for a beer.

The main square is still deserted, and the organ in St. Egidio has been joined by a powerful choir whose slow Te Deum, as broad as the Danube, floats across the square and around the church. Around and around it swirls until it finds an outlet across the ground, across the cobblestones of the square, through the streets, and over the roofs of Oberheim down to the brown water. I head down there together with the current of sound, to where a tour boat called the *Theodor Fontane* struggles against the river's current. Someone is standing by the railing and looking through binoculars at the town's facades, the poplars, and the acacias from which clumps of white flowers hang.

A girl in blue jeans is sitting on a bench in the park by the river. Her shoulders tremble; she is crying. It is spring; the girls of Oberheim are crying. A boy stands next to her with his hands in his leather jacket.

He is saying something to her, toward the current and then over it. They don't see me, though I pass close by.

Then I sit in my room and glance out at the brown waves that head toward the Black Sea. It is getting dark, the clouds have drawn nearer, beneath the windows someone is whistling, the light is no longer diffuse and translucent, it is almost opaque, then it disappears.

The radio announces that all the roads are blocked by Whitsuntide traffic. No one should travel unless absolutely necessary. I will write those thousand words, one or two more.

■ □ ■ □ ■

WRITINGS FROM AN UNBOUND EUROPE

For a complete list of titles, see the Writings from an Unbound Europe Web site at www.nupress.northwestern.edu/ue.

Words Are Something Else
DAVID ALBAHARI

Perverzion
YURI ANDRUKHOVYCH

The Second Book
MUHAREM BAZDULJ

Tworki
MAREK BIEŃCZYK

The Grand Prize and Other Stories
DANIELA CRĂSNARU

Peltse and Pentameron
VOLODYMYR DIBROVA

And Other Stories
GEORGI GOSPODINOV

The Tango Player
CHRISTOPH HEIN

In-House Weddings
BOHUMIL HRABAL

Mocking Desire
DRAGO JANČAR

A Land the Size of Binoculars
IGOR KLEKH

Balkan Blues: Writing Out of Yugoslavia
EDITED BY JOANNA LABON

The Loss
VLADIMIR MAKANIN

Compulsory Happiness
NORMAN MANEA

Border State
TÕNU ÕNNEPALU

How to Quiet a Vampire: A Sotie
BORISLAV PEKIĆ

A Voice: Selected Poems
ANZHELINA POLONSKAYA

Estonian Short Stories
EDITED BY KAJAR PRUUL AND DARLENE REDDAWAY

The Third Shore: Women's Fiction from East Central Europe
EDITED BY AGATA SCHWARTZ AND LUISE VON FLOTOW

Death and the Dervish
The Fortress
MEŠA SELIMOVIĆ

The Last Journey of Ago Ymeri
BASHKIM SHEHU

Conversation with Spinoza: A Cobweb Novel
GOCE SMILEVSKI

House of Day, House of Night
OLGA TOKARCZUK

Materada
FULVIO TOMIZZA

Shamara and Other Stories
SVETLANA VASILENKO

Lodgers
NENAD VELIČKOVIĆ